Let the
dreams
begin.

COX
COMMUNICATIONS

KiDS

FOUNDATION

From the screenwriter
of *Angels in the Outfield*
comes...

KEEPER

BY

HOLLY GOLDBERG
SLOAN

www.scobre.com

Scobre Press Corporation
2255 Calle Clara
La Jolla, CA 92037

Scobre Press books may be purchased for
educational, business or sales promotional
use.

First Scobre edition published 2002.

Edited by Debra Ginsberg
Cover Art by Anne Herlihy and Ralph King
Cover Layout by Michael Lynch

ISBN 0-9708992-3-8

www.scobre.com

To all the dreamers...

We at Scobre Press are proud to bring you another book in our "Dream Series." In case this is your first Scobre book, here's what we're all about: The goal of Scobre is to influence young people by entertaining them with books about athletes who act as role models. The moral dilemmas facing the athletes in a Scobre story run parallel to situations facing many young people today. After reading a Scobre book, our hope is that young people will be able to respond to adversity in their lives in the same heroic fashion as the athletes depicted in our books.

This book is about Sasha Lewis, a young girl whose fear of everything forces her to live her life without taking any risks. But after her best friend tricks her into joining the soccer team, her fears begin to fade, and her dreams begin to form.

We invite you now to come along with us, sit down, get comfortable, and read a book that will dare you to dream. Scobre dedicates this book to all the people who are chasing down their own dreams. We're sure that Sasha will inspire you to reach for the stars.

Here's Sasha, and "Keeper."

ONE

I have a secret. Not the kind of secret like I saw our neighbor Mrs. Higgenlooper once in the parking lot at Costco in the way back by the dumpsters and I swear I saw her kissing a man in a blue striped shirt and he wasn't Mr. Higgenlooper. And not a secret like Jenny Chow wrote nasty things on the wall in the bathroom at school with the edge of a fingernail file. This secret is about me.

I'm afraid of things.

All kinds of people are afraid of spiders and snakes (so it's okay that I'm totally and completely freaked out about those). And I know some people are afraid to fly in airplanes or go to movies with skulls on the posters. That's all considered normal. I've got bigger problems.

I'm sort of afraid of everything. Clowns. Big trees. Any room that's dark. Thunder. Firecrackers. Cats. Motorcycles. Bees. Snowballs. Most knives. Some forks. Car wash places.

Elevators. Hamsters. The guys behind the sushi counter who yell when you come in. Certain shades of purple. Alleys. Sprinkler heads. Any dog bigger than a cat and I already explained about the cats. Men in beards. Men in moustaches. Blood. Catsup (because it looks like blood). And most kinds of cheese. That's just my starter list.

I think you get the picture. Now if you think it's hard being completely and totally terrorized by a package of string cheese, think about this: I've got to hide the fact that the hair is standing up on my arms and I'm feeling like running from the room screaming when someone pulls out a piece. I've got to pretend to be normal. It's a big, big struggle. No wonder I'm tired all the time.

That's why my friend Courtney is so important. She's known me since we were in kindergarten and I refused to sit by the window (I'm uncomfortable with most heating units and there was an old radiator there). I got moved to the seat next to her, which put me as the only one not sitting in the correct position. Courtney's last name is Bilsesser and my last name is Lewis. She should have been sitting next to Ryan Cork. I think they figured that sitting alphabetically would help us learn to read easier or something. Well, I screwed that all up. Fortunately I already knew how to read when I got there. And I don't think it's right to blame me for the fact that the school had a disproportionate number of slow learners that year.

Anyway, back to Courtney. She's the kind of person who collects squirrels and baby birds when they fall out of trees and then feeds them sugar water with eye-droppers in old shoe boxes stuffed with cotton balls. And her squirrels and

2

baby birds LIVE. (Did I mention that I'm afraid of squirrels?).

Courtney has two big brothers and a mother who is a pediatric oncologist which means she treats kids with cancer so they're tough as nails in that house. Her dad works at an advertising agency doing I don't know what but he comes home all the time with tapes he makes us listen to and then we have to tell him what we think, which is always really that they stink, but we don't want to hurt his feelings so we say they're good. Courtney says he really always wanted to be a rock star but it didn't work out. How do you know that stuff about adults? He doesn't look like he could ever be a rock star. He looks like a guy losing his hair who is kind of worried a lot.

So starting in kindergarten Courtney took me on like one of her stray cats (she feeds six every day in the alley behind her house). The Bilsessers have two dogs, and three parakeets that live inside. The reason Courtney and I are best friends and closer than sisters (I don't have a sister and neither does she so this can never be put to any kind of real test), is because she thinks when I tell her that the Aspen trees have eyes in their bark and are staring at me I'm being funny. She doesn't believe I really mean it. She just smiles and gives me a little shove. I'm literally trying to keep from jumping out of my own skin and she's giggling. You gotta love her for that. I do.

So Courtney Bilsesser is kind of my anchor to anything that's normal. I live with my Grandma whose name is Reneta Bertha Beckdell. My name is Sasha Beckdell Lewis so I've got my middle name from her last name. I'm glad I didn't get the Reneta or the Bertha part. Sasha is crazy enough. I call my grandma "Nammy" and I guess it's because when I was little I couldn't grit my teeth or something. Sometimes I call her "mom" but I think she likes the "Nammy" thing better and we both know she's really my mom without me saying it. My real father was kind of a 'no-show' from the 'get go' as Nammy says. And my real Mom was never a good driver even though the accident was technically not her fault. So that has left me with Nammy. There are worse places to be left, believe me. And I know.

So it's me and the lady who loves the weather channel, anything with butterscotch, and crossword puzzles.

Courtney says that Nammy is like a cat that was de-clawed. She doesn't feel comfortable going outdoors because she doesn't have any defenses. Little does she know I'm worse than the de-clawed cat. I only go out because they have laws that say kids have to go to middle school. If they didn't I'd be parked in front of the TV with Nammy picking sunflower seed shells out of my teeth and drinking diet soda.

TWO

Our first real fight, and I mean real drag down yelling at each other and crying kind of fight was about the swim team. Obviously Courtney can swim. And obviously she's really, really good. She wanted me to join the other group of strong, v-back shaped Amazons who freeze their butts off at all hours and only have green hair to show for it. I don't think it takes Einstein to figure out that I don't have a trophy case so I'm not worrying about how to fill the thing.

The big problem is that Courtney's brothers swim. For years and years they've gotten up before the sun and silently lumbered out to the car where Mr. Bilsesser is waiting listening to National Public Radio and probably dreaming about how much better his life would have been if he was a rock star. While Ned and Wally sit in the car like two pieces of lawn furniture, Courtney's dad drives to the YMCA where they get into that freezing cold pool with all the smelly chemicals that I know for a fact cause cancer and an hour later come out with even bigger backs and thicker arms and those skinny little swimmer waists. Plus they have to wear those tiny swimsuits, which everyone says are normal in France. Afterwards they get to go to McDonalds for Sausage Egg McMuffins which is the only good part.

So everything was going along fine for us until one day Courtney says she's going out for the swim team. I immediately think about the potential health risks and how sad it is for her to have to get up early with the two big brothers when she says she wants us BOTH to do it. That's when the fighting started. And it lasted for two weeks. For fourteen straight days after the first explosion of yelling we didn't say one word to each other.

The weekends weren't as bad as the school days because even though I usually always spent every weekend with Courtney I could deal with Nammy and the weather channel and abbreviation for the airport in Mexico City (she was doing a crossword puzzle on 'world places').

But the weekdays were a real challenge because we have the same ceramics class and homeroom and we always, always, always eat lunch together. During the fourteen days of silence I just didn't eat because I would never in a million years go into that cafeteria by myself. There is no scarier place in the world than a middle school cafeteria when you don't have anyone to sit by (and remember I'm an expert on scary things).

Of course Courtney had the whole school who wanted to sit by her and the whole school who were now thrilled that she didn't have 'the Weirdo' at her sleeve. I know what they call me. I may be a big loser but I'm not totally out of it.

Every day for two weeks during what I think of as the "ice age," we never even once made eye contact. Swim season started and of course Courtney didn't just make the team she was elected captain and got to pick out the new swimsuits for everyone from a catalogue and for the first time it looked like the school had a chance to be good in a girls' sport. All the swimmers got sweatshirts that said, "Pain goes away. Pride stays forever." The first time I saw Courtney in the thing I knew she'd been brainwashed. If there was one thing I knew in my thirteen and a half years on the planet it was that pain stays forever. Any pain that's real anyway. Pride comes and goes depending on your mood and the people around you and what day of the week it is. It figures that some jock would get it all wrong.

But I didn't think Courtney looked so happy for all her success. At least the back of her head didn't look so happy. Since we were avoiding each other completely, I only was able to now and then check out her skull and I could tell that her hair was getting all splintery and brassy which I know probably didn't bother her at all but still made me feel bad inside. I bought extra conditioner at Long's drugstore and spent more time making my hair look real good just to show her where her decisions were leading.

During the two weeks I also read three books and got to know the janitor, which was a real eye-opener. His name is Jose Hernandez and he was studying to be a doctor when he lived in El Salvador, but he wanted more for his family so he moved here and now he has to pick up empty chip bags and soda cans for ten hours a day.

But he's really got a good attitude about it. Before Courtney and I had our swim team problem I never even thought about what pigs most middle school kids are. They think they use the trashcans but I've got a news flash. They don't. And I now completely understand why you can't chew gum in Singapore or wherever it is they've made it against the law. Jose's biggest battle is against chewing gum. It turns up in the craziest places. He's got a cleaner he made up himself and could probably patent and make a ton of money and retire if he could just get the world to try it. He mixes paint thinner with Windex and peanut butter. It forms this brown paste which smells like a chemical sandwich. The only real problem with the stuff is you have to work fast or it takes the finish off whatever the gum was stuck to in the first place. That's the reason the linoleum all around the school has light spots.

Jose gave me my own little can of his peanut butter cleaning paste and I took it home and put it under the sink. I told Nammy about ten times that it was cleaning stuff and marked it all over the container because sometimes when she's looking for food she can reach for just about anything.

Just when I was getting used to the hunger pains of mid-day and hanging out with Jose, Courtney walked right up to me on day fourteen at four minutes after one o'clock and said, "I don't care about you not going out for the swim team anymore."

I didn't think I heard her right and didn't even answer. She continued, "I'll never bring it up again as long as you promise that one time, just once, somewhere in the future, you'll go out for a sports team with me."

I stared at her for a while savoring my victory. She must have missed me. Either that or she felt sorry for me. I was getting even thinner now that I only ate two meals a day. And both Jose and Nammy said I looked even more pale than usual. In retrospect I probably seemed like a baby squirrel or fallen bird. It was obvious she had to pick me up.

I opened my mouth and was surprised to hear myself say simply and directly, "Okay."

We turned and silently walked to homeroom together. The ice age was over. And I didn't yet realize the enormity of the promise I made. That's the thing about promises. They're easy to make. Keeping them is another story.

THREE

Everybody has an Ashley Aiken. Ashley moved from some place in Southern California to what she liked to call "Nowhere Oregon" where we live five years ago on September 14th. A day hasn't gone by when I haven't thought about the fact that Ashley is one of those people that makes everyone's life a little worse. And I mean everyone. I know Ashley's parents and I swear even they look nervous around her.

Ashley has a voice that sounds like the brakes on my bike when I go down the steep hill in front of Del Hoff's ice cream store. It's squeaky and shrill and just all around annoying. She's an only child, which I can't be against on principle because I'm in the same boat. But I don't have two people waiting at all times for my every command as if they worked for me. I don't even have one since mostly I'm the person bringing Nammy things. I'm not complaining because no matter what anyone thinks of Nammy, as long as the dirty dishes are loaded into the machine and her soda still has bubbles, she's in her green chair minding her own business.

The good news about Ashley is she doesn't go to school with me. She's better than that. Courtney and I go to Eleanor Roosevelt Middle School. Ashley's parents got some kind of special permission for her to go across town to Franklin Middle School. Franklin was built only ten years ago and all the classrooms are big and have a TV that hangs on a pole in the corner and bright-colored furniture made out of curvy plastic. Roosevelt's been around forever and every room has that smell of layers and layers of old paint and floor wax. All our desks are made of wood and have stuff carved in the top and wobbly legs because just about everything's been repaired a million times.

So fortunately, I only see Ashley in the mornings when I pass by her huge house which is at the end of my block. Nammy and I live in the smallest house on the street which is just fine because it's only the two of us and because I'm afraid of large structures. Plus Nammy's lived here forever and she says if we had to afford to get a place now we'd be in a trailer park or something.

Every two weeks when Nammy gets around to looking through the stack of bills next to the green chair she says, "We're hanging on by our fingernails, sister." We just barely squeak by on the social security checks I get for not having a Mom anymore combined with the social security checks she gets for not having a husband anymore. If I could get the cable service to black out the Home Shopping Channel everything would probably ease up for us. Sometimes Nammy sees things for sale in the middle of the day and even though it's stuff we don't need, and stuff that we probably don't even really want, she just can't help herself. That's why we have three automatic cat box cleaners (but no cat), all kinds of electric can openers and food slicers, and enough cubic zirconia jewelry to start our own boutique.

Nammy says it's important to have good costume jewelry in the house in case we're robbed at gunpoint and they want our valuables. The plan is to hand over a bag of the cubic zirconia instead of the real stuff. The only flaw in Nammy's thinking is we don't have any real stuff and if you took a look around our place I don't think you'd find this shocking. But Nammy won't hear a word of my logic and when she starts talking about gunpoint and robbers I'm up for any plan she has.

At night when I'm lying in bed worrying about things like robbers with pistols or a possible invasion of the area by flying grasshoppers, the only thing that helps me calm down is the knowledge that any robber with half a brain would go to Ashley Aiken's. They have two brand new Sport Utility Vehicles in their driveway and every electronic device for sale in the Sharper Image catalog is sitting in their living room. That's the flip side of being a show-off. You make yourself a target.

Ashley is one of those only children who does endless activities. She plays the piano and takes ice-skating lessons and does whatever sport is in season. But she's not like Courtney. When Courtney runs she looks like a deer. Her head sort of floats forward and there is so much spring in her legs you can't believe she's really hitting the ground. When Ashley runs she looks like she was hired to kill insects. Every foot is planted hard and her face sets into what looks like the mask of anger. Plus she makes all kinds of weirdo grunting sounds.

I know this because when I was smaller Ashley thought that a fun thing to do was to chase me home. If she saw me rounding the corner on the sidewalk on my way back from Courtney's, she'd bound out of her house and come at me, sometimes hurling rotten apples from the Wallerstein's yard right at my head. I tried all kinds of tactics to get her to stop, including writing her a mean note which I claimed was from the police. I put it in her mailbox with a stamp and everything but nothing worked.

Finally I just started walking home the long way, going an extra two blocks north and passing the scariest dog in the world (it doesn't matter that he's behind a fence because he would rip my legs right off in a nanosecond if he ever got the chance). But that didn't mean Ashley was out of my life forever. It just meant I didn't have to worry about the rotten apple assault for a while.

FOUR

Eighth grade was supposed to be hard but so far it didn't really seem that way. They made a lot of noise about preparing us for the future, which means high school, but from what I could tell the people who aren't prepared never are, no matter what they do. Calvin Montgomery always loses his backpack every year, and brainiacs like Mindy Shik always do more extra-credit assignments than the teachers can even come up with.

The year really is different only because we have to do the science fair. They talk about the thing as if they really believe one of us is going to clone a sheep or something. I bet there's not a kid in my whole grade that will end up with a job in science. And I would put five dollars on the possibility that we've got a whole mess of kids who will end up in food services. I don't see any kind of cooking fair being planned. So much for all that preparation for our future.

Courtney has no science fair anxiety because her mother

is a doctor. Plus Courtney's whole idea of fun is growing things and watching the progress. My idea of a good time is killing germs, especially since I read about that flesh eating virus and the recent outbreak of tuberculosis. For awhile there I was washing my hands about forty times a day. Then I read that people who do that are crazy and I started to go crazy just thinking about how crazy I was being and I had to make myself stop. I still put a paper towel over the doorknob when I turn it to get out of a toilet in a gas station but I don't think anyone's going to lock me up for that.

Courtney and I both have Ms. Biculos as our science teacher even though we don't have class the same period. Ms. Biculos wears high heels to school everyday and dark suits that make her look like a flight attendant. She's only in her second year of teaching and hasn't figured out yet that she should be in track shoes and ugly pants like the other science teachers. Ms. Biculos came to us all the way from Florida after working in a real lab where she did stuff for the space program. Shelly Wetterling said she got fired when a new satellite blew up which cost like a billion dollars. Shelly said she was one of the only girl scientists so it figures they'd blame her. I'm really curious what Ms. Biculos did to make it explode and I want to ask her all the time when I'm in class but I don't want to embarrass her so I'm just waiting for the chance for us to be alone one day and for her to be in a confessional mood.

The first Friday in October they made us turn in our science fair proposals. Courtney is growing brine shrimp in water with different levels of salt. I would never, ever, in a million, trillion years do this. I can't stand the smell of fish,

I'm afraid of shrimp (don't they look like they could bite and what's the story with those tails?) and everyone knows that water projects are twice as much work as land ones. I tried to talk Courtney out of it and she patiently explained that brine shrimp are really tiny and can only be seen under a microscope. That's when I thought she might be on to something. It wasn't like she was raising kittens. No one would know if they were growing or not. She could make a whole lot of it up if things didn't work out. After I told her I was onto her scheme she just laughed. I really hope she's not interested for real because that just wouldn't be right.

The first proposal I submitted for the fair was rejected. The second one even got me in trouble. My first idea was to work with the guy they hired to spray the bug killer once a month on the walls in back of the cafeteria. He drives a pick-up truck with a dented metal spider on the door and usually wears a blue plastic suit with yellow kitchen gloves and what I know for a fact are swim goggles when he's spraying. I'm sure I could have worked out a nice project with him and even learned something about toxic chemicals but they wouldn't hear of it.

My second idea was to use surveillance to determine how most teachers actually spent their school time while not in the classroom. Were they in the teacher's lounge? The bathroom? The back parking lot sneaking cigarettes? Did any of them spend time together? Could you make any connection to what they did while not teaching with how happy they seemed in the classroom? And I had a very solid plan where I was going to put these collars on their ankles that were designed to keep track of hunting dogs. I saw them for sale in the back of a magazine at the dentist's office. I guess it was kind of a big project but that's not what they had a problem with.

Ms. Biculos got all pink in the face when she read my proposal paragraph and called out my name in the way that instantly says you're in more trouble than when you have to spin that goofy karma wheel that has choices like "Get a free candy bar" or "Stay after school and clean the mouse cages." Right in front of the whole class she asked me if I'd shown my proposal to anyone and I don't think she believed me when I said no. I didn't want to go into Nammy and the fact that no one has looked at my homework ever in my entire life so I just kept quiet. She made me go see Mr. Hockstatter who is the principal and then he got all pink in the face and said he'd never had a cigarette in the back parking lot, which was weird, because who ever said he did?

After that they decided to assign me a science project which everyone knows is what they wanted to do all along. I'm growing mold on bread in different light conditions. Just the idea of it makes me want to throw up. We've been growing mold in different light conditions in our kitchen for as long as I can remember and I haven't learned one thing from it and obviously neither has Nammy.

FIVE

Before I really knew what happened swim season was over and girls had basketball or gymnastics to pick from if they wanted to go out for a sport. I am one of the only girls in our whole grade that can't do a cartwheel or a handstand so it had to be clear right away to Courtney that gymnastics was out. Just to make sure she got the picture I climbed up onto the balance beam after PE class on the Monday before try-outs. I fell off on my first step forward and the school nurse said she thought I'd sprained my ankle. I hobbled around for a few days but unfortunately it got better.

This left basketball. As a sport, basketball requires all kinds of skills that you can't just learn in one day even if you wanted to. And I didn't want to.

Courtney doesn't even try at basketball and of course she's one of the best girls in our grade. She's goofed around with her brothers since she was a toddler and she can shoot from anywhere and the ball just goes in. She always looks sort of surprised as if it was some kind of accident. She can jump better than all of the girls and most of the boys. If you want to know the truth, she's sort of a natural player. So Courtney tried to talk me into going out for the basketball squad and this time I had the good sense not to just say 'no' but to play along with her delusions. Any fool would see I wouldn't be helping the team.

Coach Moshofsky has been at Eleanor Roosevelt for a million years and really loves basketball. She also really loves winning so I knew my plan was good. When I walked into the gym on the first afternoon of the three-day try-out her face squeezed up like she'd just bit into a sour tangerine. Courtney was at my side but Coach Moshofsky realized the second she saw my thin legs in the oversized gym shorts that I wasn't there as a friend. I was there as a competitor. I could tell right away that the idea frightened her.

Over the next three afternoons I jammed my right finger so bad it had to be put in a splint, cracked the glass in one of the high gymnasium windows (bad pass), missed every shot I took, and accidentally tripped fellow teammate Jessica Pendergast, causing her to miss the entire season with torn knee cartilage. There was no question of the kind of damage I would cause if I continued.

But Coach Moshofsky didn't want to do anything to upset Courtney. And she knew how much it meant to her for me to walk away from the experience with my head held high. So instead of just cutting me, she called me into her office at the end of her third day. Courtney was breathless, "Coach wants to see you. Sasha, I think you have a shot."

Part of my strategy was to act like I really cared. I tried to look as sincere as possible when I said, "I've got my fingers crossed."

Coach Moshofsky's office was small and filled with dusty junk from years of sporting events, including a stuffed hog holding a blue basketball and a bunch of old sports calendars and sweatbands. It smelled like wet socks and vitamins with iron.

"Have a seat, Sasha."

I sat down in the one available chair and looked straight at the linoleum floor.

"You put a lot of effort into your basketball try-out."

I nodded.

"In the past I've never seen you put in much effort in PE class."

I shrugged.

"I think the other girls were impressed."

I'd made an impression, that was for sure. Coach continued, "If I can't find room for you on the squad, I don't want you to feel bad."

I tried to make sure there was zero joy in my voice:

"I'm not going to make the team?"

Coach cleared her throat, "I don't think so."

I looked up and was surprised to see the Coach Moshofsky actually felt sorry for me. Truly sorry. I seized the opportunity.

My lower lip trembled as I said, "If I can't be on the team I don't think I'll be able to play basketball in regular PE class. It would be too painful."

And so Coach Moshofsky and I cut a deal. In order to protect my fragile mental health, I was excused from PE for the rest of the term which gave me a whole free period every day to catch up with Jose the Janitor.

Jose had enrolled in night school and was studying to be a nurse. If he couldn't be a doctor he wanted to at least get his hand back in medicine. I spent the first fifteen minutes of my free period in the supply closet every day testing him on the stuff he learned the night before. That's why I now know the difference between a feeding cup and a feeding beaker, and can answer the all-important question: "How many fluid ounces will the standard male bedside incontinent device hold?"

So for nine solid weeks I ate Milk Duds, went on-line to my favorite websites in the library, and studied the nursing catalog. I'd never had it this good. And Courtney was okay with it because I'd tried to play a sport.

At the end of the term, when I saw the "PASS" in the space next to Physical Education, I was very proud. For a brief moment I thought maybe they were right. Pain goes away. Pride stays forever.

SIX

Courtney's basketball team came in second in the league and everyone said that if Jessica Pendergast hadn't torn her ligaments in try-outs they might have won the whole darn thing. Courtney didn't seem to care, even when she got an award with a gold seal for being Most Valuable Player. It came in a black plastic frame that looked like real wood from far away and had the signatures of Coach Moshofsky and Mr. Hockstatter.

But Courtney had a bunch of them already and she didn't even put it out on display. It ended up in a box in the back of her closet with a mess of colored ribbons and a math award from sixth grade. I was the only one who ever took the stuff out and that was when she was in the shower or in the alley feeding the crazy cats and wouldn't think I was snooping around.

The Bilsesser's was the only place besides my own house where I would ever spend the night. Even though they had two dogs the size of pack mules, and a cage with parakeets that obviously wanted to peck my eyes out if they were given a chance, I was able to calm down enough to sleep for at least part of the night. I'd usually wake up before the sun even came up and twice I got a bad rash, but it helped that Courtney's mother was a real doctor. I figured if I stopped breathing or one of the dogs bit me at least they wouldn't have to call 911.

It was February and I was sleeping over on a Saturday night when Courtney stopped channel-surfing and made us actually watch part of a soccer game on the Spanish language channel. I should have figured out something was up but I innocently believed her when she said how big the stadium was and what cool orange shirts they were wearing. We'd stayed up late watching all kinds of junk on TV the night before and then gotten yelled at by Courtney's mom, who seemed to think there was some direct link from the television to our minds rotting.

She and Nammy had nothing in common. In all the time I'd known Dr. Bilsesser I don't remember her once sitting with her feet up, and I don't think I've ever seen her do a crossword puzzle or suck on a butterscotch drop. She's always moving. And even when she's talking and asking us questions half the time she answers them herself and jumps to the next topic before you can even get going on the first one. If Nammy asks something she waits for the answer as if I was an important reporter on her favorite television show. She always wants to know what I think and listens even when I'm just making stuff up which is about half the time. I could get a bat and go downtown and hit a bunch of people in the mall and come home and tell Nammy and she'd listen and then tell me they deserved it. You get the picture. She keeps the curtains closed twenty-four-seven. I'm kind of the light around the place.

Which isn't to say Dr. and Mr. Bilsesser don't think Courtney's great, but they've got Wally and Ned and the two drooling dogs, and they work at jobs that they're still thinking about when they come home. They exercise every day and are always rushing to a yoga class or the running club and they eat fresh food not stuff that's been in cans or frozen so they go to the market every two seconds and the dry cleaners. Plus they have to attend neighborhood meetings and parties where people use little napkins and eat stuff on toothpicks. Nammy doesn't do any of that so she's got lots of time.

As a rule I don't eat anything stuck on a toothpick because when I was in the second grade I sucked too hard on a fudgesicle stick after I'd been chewing on it trying to get the very last part of the chocolate taste off. It broke in two and one of the pieces went straight back and got stuck in my throat and I had to go to the hospital. I've never seen Nammy so upset and she was crying and swearing all at the same time and she never drives because of what happened to Mom but she tried to and the car wouldn't start so Mr. Wallerstein from down the street took us.

By the time Nammy had filled out the forms and they finally got the Doctor in the room I'd swallowed the piece of stuck wood. I didn't even know it. All that was left was a big scratch in the back of my throat and so instead of giving me any medicine they made Nammy take two blue pills to calm herself down. She got so tired she fell asleep in the taxi going home (which wasn't really her fault because it took twenty-five minutes for him to show up). Me and the driver (who was really nice) had to kind of drag her inside because we just couldn't wake her up. Afterwards the taxi guy stayed for a cup of hot chocolate and wouldn't take any money which was so nice I couldn't believe it. Nammy said it gave her faith in the system but she didn't mean the system of taxi drivers she meant the system of hospitals I think.

After all that happened we never had any kind of ice cream in the house anymore. Nammy said we just didn't need the aggravation. I'm okay with that because ice cream isn't as good as chocolate in my book, or custard or most kinds of pies.

SEVEN

So the first clue about the soccer situation was the game we watched in Spanish with Argentina and Mexico. The second thing to happen was Courtney started acting crazy after school. We'd be walking home, like always, talking about Duncan Frye's irritating laugh or Mary Tignanello's new braces, and she'd suddenly see something out of the corner of her eye and shriek. Since she'd never been afraid of anything in the whole seven and half years that I'd known her, this was big news. It goes without saying that if she was scared, I was out of my mind. And so we'd end up running. And she didn't stop right away. She ran for blocks. The first time it happened I lost my history book and forty-three cents. But I didn't think twice when she said she'd seen a huge spider. Maybe she'd finally gotten some common sense.

Then she saw hairy men in the shadows. Birds with big claws. A bat on a telephone pole. Pretty soon it seemed like we were running at least half of the way home every day. In the beginning I was out of breath and bright red for about two hours afterwards. But after a few weeks of the constant mad dashes I hardly noticed the difference. It had always taken us forty-five minutes to get to her house. Now we were in the front door in less than twenty. With the extra time we had before our favorite soap opera started, Courtney took to kicking an old volleyball against the wall of her garage. I sat in the grass and watched. Sometimes the ball would go off all crazy and end up in the yard next to me and my magazines. When this happened Courtney would yell for me to kick it back.

And I still didn't put two and two together. I ran every day and kicked a ball and didn't realize that she had me in training. But that wasn't all. She suddenly became this insane hockey fan. She talked about hockey all the time and had a favorite team and she'd draw these diagrams on notebook paper and talk about the forwards and the goalie and how they passed to each other and moved the puck around and what it meant to be "off-sides." I was bored out of my mind but figured it was something she'd get over like a sore throat or a new tee-shirt or something. Now I can't believe the planning that went into the whole scheme.

Her brother Wally came home from high school every day and he started kicking that old volleyball for about fifteen minutes, too. And when his kicks went bad I had to go twice as far to get them. Wally started giving me advice when I booted the stupid thing back. He'd yell at me to put my whole body into it and all kinds of stuff about 'follow through.' I figured he was just a natural boss because he was always telling us what to do anyway.

But then the other brother, Ned, got in on the action. Ned was bigger than Wally and moved slower. Where Wally talks all the time and makes people laugh, Ned keeps more to himself and looks serious. So when Ned started telling me stuff I got scared. His upper lip lately had this layer of brown hair that wasn't a real moustache but wasn't not a moustache. And I'm afraid of people with moustaches. Plus Ned is the oldest boy I've ever really talked to. He's got friends who can drive cars so he gets dropped off after school like he's a grown-up and he's always got a bag of cold French fries from some drive-thru place they stopped at on the way home.

At first Ned just stood in the driveway and watched. But then he started telling me to drop my head a little when I kicked the ball and to put more guts in my foot. I didn't have any idea what he was talking about. The whole thing was just crazy.

And I can't even say I was the one to figure it all out. It was Clyde. He lives two blocks from me and Nammy. I first met him a long time ago when I thought a big rust-colored dog was going to attack me and I ran up and hid on Clyde's prop-erty. He came out and crouched down next to his broken porch swing demanding to know what the problem was. I told him about the killer dog loose on the sidewalk and he got on the phone and called some lady who lived down the street and she came right away to claim the thing as if he were a winning lottery ticket. After that I sat with Clyde and he smoked ciga-rettes and told me how he was in World War II and how rotten it was to get old and how he had been married three times and how his kids were all sort of jerks.

I made a point of checking in on him once a week after that because I'm used to old people because of Nammy and I didn't care that he smells funny and really, really needs to clip his fingernails more often.

The best thing about Clyde is that he's just always disappointed with everyone and everything and he feels okay talking about it. He's had cancer and had an operation to take it out of his bowel (which I think is just the grossest sounding word) and even though they told him it didn't look good he didn't believe them and now it's been seven years and he feels as bad as he did before he had anything officially wrong with him. Feeling good isn't something he's ever been comfortable with.

Right after his cancer problem he went back east to see one of his lazy sons and he was run over by a bakery van when he stepped off the curb into traffic. It wasn't his fault and they thought he'd never make it but he did and now he has a steel stick in one leg and a steel pin in the other which is why he walks funny although I never knew him when he walked good.

So Clyde was sitting with me on the porch and he said I didn't look as pale as normal and I said I'd been outside kicking the ball back to Courtney and Wally and even Ned for a while and he got this funny look on his face and said:

"They're up to something."

EIGHT

He was right. The very next day after ceramics class Courtney couldn't even bring herself to look at me when she says oh-so-casually, "Spring sports are coming up. I thought we'd go out for soccer."

I swallowed hard. Soccer was a sport for girls who had thick legs and strong bodies and who weren't afraid of balls whizzing around like cannon projectiles. People kicked at other people on purpose and slammed their heads into leather and each other. You had to wear cleats which were so scary, and molded plastic pieces strapped to your shins. Soccer players ran around in fields like packs of wild animals scrambling after what in ancient times had been the inflated stomach of a goat. It was barbaric.

All I said back was, "Soccer?"

Courtney still wasn't even looking at me.

"Yeah. It's super fun. And I think you'll be real good

31

at it."

My idea of super fun is a field trip to a security systems company. And the list of things I'm real good at could fit on a postage stamp. I stopped dead in my tracks.

"Really?"

She had to meet my gaze. And when she did she looked guilty.

"You'll tryout—right?"

That night when I was looking through the newspaper and cutting out all the articles about accidents (I glue them into a huge scrapbook I've kept for the last five years), I figured soccer try-outs could end up being a good thing. I'd never played the game in my life so there was no way I would make the team. And that meant that with any luck I had a chance to weasel out of gym class again. The secret would be to really try. Sports types were real suckers for sweaty effort.

When I finished pasting the article about the car crash at the railroad crossing next to the small story about the man who got his shirt stuck in the printing press and lost two fingers, the doorbell rang. Nammy yelled not to answer it because that was our policy, especially if it was dark outside. The only problem was that now that her hearing wasn't so good, she rarely spoke anymore; she yelled all of her instructions. So at the top of her lungs she bellowed for me to not answer the door. It was loud enough to be heard down the street. And it was followed by Courtney's voice coming through the front door, "It's me! It's just Courtney!"

So of course I answered it. Courtney was standing on the doormat with a bag in her hand. Her face was flushed from the cold night air. I could see Mr. Bilsesser seated behind the wheel of his car at the curb and I think I saw Wally in the backseat but I wasn't sure. It might have been one of their huge dogs.

"Here. We got you these. They were on sale so it's no big deal."

Before I could even respond she'd pushed a plastic bag with a cardboard box inside into my arms. She turned with a wave and in a few effortless strides was back at her car. I shut the door because Nammy was still yelling:

"Don't answer the door!"

I went straight to my room and sat down on the bed.

The shoes were black leather and had three white stripes along the sides. I flipped them over and stared at the hard white plastic soles. They were studded with raised round bumps like an oversized kid's Lego. I held them in my hands as if they were artifacts from an historic dig. They may as well have been. Nammy and I didn't own anything athletic unless you count her fourth husband Rayford's old bowling ball which is still in the hall closet. I never really knew Rayford and from the sound of it either did Nammy. He was only around for six months and then dropped dead one day at Stan's Donut Shop right after he bit into a honey-glazed twist. He left Nammy with all kinds of bills for things she never knew he'd bought, the bowling ball, and a metal detector that didn't work.

I held the shoes right up to my nose and inhaled big. They smelled like cattle. Or at least what I imagine cattle smell like. They had a strong, outdoor, somewhat masculine odor. I couldn't help myself. As much as I hated the idea of soccer and all things related to the sport, I wanted to try them on.

I was surprised that they made me seem a lot taller. It must be because of the cleats. I clattered around my room for awhile certain I'd get a blister or strain something but it was useless. They fit perfectly. Finally after an hour I picked up the telephone and called Courtney. She answered on the first ring.

"Bilsesser residence."

I skipped right to what she wanted to hear.

"I'm wearing the shoes."

Her joyful shriek was numbing.

NINE

Most of the stuff I own comes from garage sales or second hand stores. Nammy's right that you can get good stuff for cheap at places like the Salvation Army and Goodwill. We've been going there our whole lives. At least I have anyway. But that doesn't mean I want the entire world to know we shop 'used.' That's why I got all worked up when Ashley Aiken saw me and Nammy head into the Salvation Army on Ferry Street on Saturday. It's one thing to go there because you *want* to. It's another to shop there because you *have* to.

Ashley was waiting impatiently in her mother's brand new car when Nammy and I got off the bus and came down the sidewalk. If I'd seen her sooner I could have told Nammy I needed to go to the bathroom and then got her into El Sombrero for some chips and salsa. Or I might have claimed I saw a black cat so we'd have to cross the street for sure. But it was too late. I didn't see Ashley's slick sheet of blond hair until we turned toward the doorway and I had a view of the parking lot.

As soon as she saw me she started to laugh. No matter

who you are, or what you're doing, when someone laughs at you and you haven't told a joke or made a face or goofed on yourself, it makes you feel rotten. You just can't help but wonder if you didn't zip up your pants or something. Ashley laughed and she laughed hard. Then she pantomimed throwing a rotten apple at my head and mouthed "See 'ya around!"

My face was all red and I felt sort of dizzy as we came through the thrift store's front door. Mrs. Aiken was standing at the counter arguing with the wide woman at the register. It figures Ashley's mom would have some problem. I was thinking she bought something and didn't look carefully and then went home and found the catsup stain or the buttons missing. Everybody knows you can't return stuff to a second hand store and I momentarily felt good thinking she wasn't a critical shopper. But I had it wrong. Her problem was she'd dropped off four bags of clothing in the back and she didn't believe they'd written down the right amount on the donation slip. She was loud as she said, "You wouldn't understand, that much I get, but this is important for TAX reasons. For the DEDUCTION."

The register lady gave her a look that said she wouldn't spit on her if she were on fire. Meanwhile a line was forming.

Nammy hadn't seen Ashley in the car and didn't see her mother at the counter. And she wouldn't know who they were even if she had seen them. She had eyes only for an orange juice dispenser on the rear shelf with a rainbow of dancing citrus figures. We never drank orange juice and we had too many pitchers already but that wouldn't stop Nammy. Walking in her slow, awkward way, she headed straight to the back. I lingered at the front pretending to be interested in a rocking chair because I was hoping the register lady might haul off and slug Ashley's mother. Instead she just hissed at her:

"You have to take it up with the man in the back. I just do sales."

Ashley's mother pressed on:

"If you add up what we paid for those clothes it comes to literally thousands and thousands of dollars!"

She held out a slip of paper as if it were evidence at a murder trial. It was clear this was the crime of the century:

"He wrote a hundred dollars. For everything. For all four bags!"

The people in line behind her were starting to get restless. A man with a cane blew his nose hard. A lady with a walker pushed it back and forth like she was revving an engine.

But before the cashier could make her next move the front door of the store flew open and Ashley appeared. She didn't step one foot into the room, bellowing instead from her position on the edge of the sidewalk:

"What is taking so long?!"

Mrs. Aiken's head snapped around. It was clear who called the shots. Mrs. Aiken suddenly reached across the counter and grabbed a black magic marker. While all of us watched she defiantly changed the 'one' on the donation receipt to a 'five'. She then headed toward Ashley, cooing in an unnatural voice, "I'm coming, dear."

Ashley shot me a parting look that said 'loser' and headed back down the sidewalk to their car. It was only then that I heard the sound. A clattering, clicking sound. I moved to

TEN

I think what happened the next day was totally Ashley Aiken's fault. On the bus ride home I was real quiet and I didn't even take one of Nammy's licorice squares which come all the way from England and are wrapped in silver paper. She usually only buys them on special occasions. That's when she figured out something was wrong. Nammy was chewing on a big piece of black candy, happily holding the juice dispenser with the dancing citrus family, when she asked me:

"Are you sick or something?"

I couldn't tell her about Ashley and her mother and how I didn't want to ever go in the Salvation Army again. How could I buy clothes there when it was now possible I'd end up owning some old shirt of Ashley Aiken's? I'd rather die. So I just slouched deeper into the bus seat and shrugged as I said, "Have we ever *given* anything to the Salvation Army or do we only buy stuff there?"

Nammy snorted through her nose.

"Of course we give them things. All the time."

I didn't say that I never once remembered us donating anything and the fact that you couldn't close any of our closets or drawers probably didn't look good for her position.

She must have thought about it because the next morning she packed up two large garbage bags of stuff and loaded them into my old red wagon. I offered to help but she must have known I didn't really mean it because she said she'd rather walk to the drop-off box by herself. She never left the house two days in a row so I knew she was making some kind of statement.

The grocery store on Franklin Boulevard has one of those little wooden houses in the corner of the parking lot that look like they belong in a pre-school but have a swinging door on one side of the roof and are for making charity donations. According to Nammy, she had placed her purse next to the trash bags and she was distracted when she dumped the stuff in. It was only when she looked back at the completely empty red wagon did she realize she'd just donated her purse to the Salvation Army.

A more regular person might have just walked to the pay phone on the other side of the parking lot and called the Salvation Army. But it was Sunday, and Nammy figured no one would answer the phone. So she decided to take matters into her own hands. She'd go in after the purse.

She positioned my old red wagon right underneath the swinging roof door and climbed up. She's stronger than I thought because I was shocked that she got herself through the swinging door into the drop off box. She said she was lucky it was filled with old clothes because she sort of tumbled in once the bulk of her weight went through the door. It was pretty dark inside but she found her purse right away. She then pushed all of the donated stuff up to the roof door to make it easier for her to get back through.

What Nammy didn't know was that there had been a problem lately of homeless people stealing stuff from the drop-off boxes. I don't really understand how a homeless person can be stealing if the Salvation Army's goal is to help the people who are homeless but I guess they want them to come to the store and show that they're desperate like the rest of us do.

So anyway, there had been this problem and the police had been told and now they drove by a few times a day to see if anything was going on. That's why they were there when Nammy's head popped out of the donation box.

I was in my room trying to do the assigned reading for science which was killing me because it was about astronomy and I get really upset thinking about the stars and the planets and the universe and the idea that it stops or doesn't stop and it always makes me feel so small and helpless and sweaty. So I already had a stomach ache when the phone rang and a voice said he was calling from the police station and they had my Nammy in custody.

I have an uncle but he's really only a half-uncle because he and my Mom had different fathers. He lives in Boston and calls Nammy every year on Christmas but otherwise we don't hear from him and Nammy says he was always more trouble than he was worth but I think that was because his father was the one Nammy liked the best and he left her one day a long, long time ago after he played golf and he just never came back.

I've only seen Uncle Arnold twice in my life and I don't remember either time. I guess he's real smart because he works in a lab with genes and up until about a year ago I thought that meant he made pants because we hadn't studied genes yet in science and no one ever explains anything around here. You just get it from hanging around and figuring it out yourself. I think Uncle Arnold might have more to do with Nammy if I weren't in the picture because my guess is he doesn't want to end up raising me so he stays away.

So when I hung up the phone I thought about trying to find the number for Uncle Arnold because this seemed like a family emergency. But then I realized even if I could find the number, which wasn't very likely, what would he be able to do? He was on the other side of the country in his gene lab and I was here in Oregon.

I put on my jacket with the big hood because I didn't want anyone to see me going into the police station and I silently cursed the Aikens for all the trouble they caused. I took all the money in my savings box, which was twenty-three dollars, and I ran straight to Clyde's house.

ELEVEN

He came to the door right away and it was one of those days where he'd missed big patches when he shaved so there were whole parts of his chin and cheeks that had thickets of white stubble. It looked like a crummy lawn-mowing job. Clyde kind of lives for bad news so he smiled big when I told him that my Nammy was in jail. We spent about a half an hour trying to find his car keys, which turned out to be in his pocket the whole time, and then we took off in his big old Chrysler.

Clyde is the worst driver in the world. He goes real fast and then real slow and he can't see very well so all kinds of things are hazards to him and real hazards he mostly doesn't even notice. He slammed on the brakes for a yellow dog, which was actually a fire hydrant, and then he almost ran over a kid on a skateboard who was in a crosswalk. He nearly took a slice out of every parked car and where there were side-view mirrors on his Chrysler there are now only metal stubs as proof he can't judge a lane. Because he's eighty-eight years old he has to take the driver's test every year but I have no clue how he's managed to pass. If I were in charge he wouldn't make it out of the parking lot.

By the time we got to the police station I was breathing funny and seeing spots. I was worried sick imagining Nammy in all kinds of trouble. Instead I found her drinking hot cider with her new friends, Officer Crowley and Officer Morales. She was helping the desk clerk do a crossword puzzle and giving suggestions on junk food preparation to the office manager. She looked disappointed, not relieved, when I walked through the door and didn't even try to hide it from me.

It turned out that once the officers heard about Nammy's five husbands and her streak of incredibly bad luck (which probably included a few words about me ending up on her doorstep), they were all ears. No one seemed to care anymore about the Salvation Army box and they for sure weren't going to press any charges. She was now their new mascot.

Clyde and I stood around like party poopers as Nammy finally gathered up her things to go. When she finally stood up she had a pair of old green nylon underpants stuck to the back of her jacket which must have come from the drop-off box. They all got a big laugh when she peeled them off and the static made that kind of crackle sound.

Once we were in the Chrysler and the excitement died down Nammy suddenly started moaning about all the injuries she got in the fall inside the box. Her back was killing her and her hip felt funny and she said even her vision was all messed up. Clyde chimed in that maybe she was about to get a stroke and that really set her off. His driving didn't help. He went through a red light and made a wrong turn onto a one-way street and Nammy didn't just yell at him, she actually started moving her hands around like bent windmills and twice hit the steering wheel. By the time we got home I felt like I was the one who was an old lady.

Once we were inside the front door Nammy asked me about a million questions about Clyde and wanted to know why I didn't call Courtney's family to help. I didn't really have an answer. She was surprised I had known Clyde for three years and never said anything to her about him and she looked at me funny like now she thought I was some kind of stranger. I didn't tell her that when the police called I had gotten so scared I kind of lost my mind and I just ran out the front door. I went to Clyde's because once I hit the sidewalk I didn't know what to do and his house was just right there in the distance.

After all the questions she said she had to rest because she was more tired than she ever remembered being and she went straight to her room. I went to the kitchen because I hadn't eaten anything yet all day and now it was the afternoon. I poured myself a bowl of cereal even though I knew we didn't have any milk and I made a little plate with celery sticks with peanut butter spread inside which is one of the main things I live on. I took my food into the bathroom and started a hot tub and then added dishwashing liquid because that makes a lot of good bubbles. This is what I do when I just want to feel that everything is okay in the world. Plus I'm cold a lot and it's the fastest way to heat myself up.

I put my food on the edge of the porcelain tub and then

I don't know why but I got in with all my clothes on. They separated away from my body and floated, swishing up against my skin like wet leaves or the small hands of a child. I wondered where the boy I would grow up to marry was right at this very moment and I thought it might be possible that somewhere he was taking a bath too, or maybe eating cereal without milk or celery with peanut butter. I wondered if we already had a connection and didn't know it and later if we'd be able to link up the dots which would form some kind of line that would lead us back to some place where it was possible we were thinking the same thing at the same time. That's what happens I guess, when you spend a lot of time alone or with someone who's sixty-five years older than you are. You do a lot of dreaming.

TWELVE

Monday morning I wrapped my new soccer shoes in old Christmas tissue and took them to school in my backpack. Courtney was jumpy and excited all day, which is just not like her. She'd put a lot of effort into her plan and it was obvious she was feeling pretty good about it. I asked around and found out that a lot of the girls going out for the team had played since something called 'K-league,' which meant kindergarten I guess. So they'd been on a soccer field for eight years. It was music to my ears.

After our last class Courtney and I got our things and went to the gym to change. I felt like a spy because I wasn't really there for the same reason as the other twenty-six girls and since I had to hide my true feelings it made me feel dangerous and like a risk-taker which is about as far from the real me as you can get.

Coach Moshofsky didn't coach soccer. That was my first disappointment. It hadn't occurred to me that I'd have to deal with someone else during try-outs. And even if I had given it some thought I'd never have figured they'd get some guy with an accent from Europe who actually knew what he was doing.

There wasn't anybody in our school like Otto. When I think about it, there wasn't anybody I'd ever seen in real life like him either. Otto Czernin looked like he belonged on TV selling toothpaste with special whiteners or a fancy sports car. He was twenty-three and tall, with all kinds of brown curly hair and yesterday's beard growth. His eyes were gray with little carrot colored slices swirling around that made him look like a wild dog or a circus performer. His body was one hundred percent muscle and his legs were so strong they would scare people. They scared me anyway.

Otto had played for two years for the Hungarian Olympic team and then he'd hurt himself and had knee surgery and after that his soccer career was over. So he came to America to study sports medicine but that didn't work out and he ended up in our town where he was getting a degree in electrical engineering at the University. He had one semester left and then he was going back to Eastern Europe to make their lights brighter or something.

But Otto loved soccer and he missed it. So when some guy he knew at the shoe store said our middle school needed a coach he decided he had time in the afternoons and why not get paid a little money (very little) to help some American girls learn something about the most beautiful sport in the world.

Courtney walked out onto the field with me a few steps behind her and the second she saw him, all of her thinking changed. She was cheerfully going on about how well she thought I'd do and a whole lot of other pep talk stuff when she suddenly stopped mid-sentence. Her eyes were riveted on Otto.

Now I've known boys like Evan Scheuer or David Dewey who Courtney liked for a day or a week or maybe even a month but it's never any big deal and she doesn't even talk about it really. That is until Otto came into the picture. He had more appeal for all of us thirteen-year-old girls, than we ever knew a member of the opposite sex could possess. He was, in short, the coolest guy we'd ever met. And it took us all about thirty seconds to figure it out. It took Courtney one glance.

As she walked toward the sidelines of the field where he was standing it suddenly didn't matter if I played soccer or not. What mattered was holding a clipboard, wearing a faded blue sweatshirt and baggy shorts.

After Otto introduced himself he asked us all to run four laps around the field to warm up. He said it would give him a chance to take a quick look at our general condition. In the gym, Courtney had said that if we were going to do any running she'd be right next to me and we'd just go at whatever pace I wanted. That was now ancient history. When Courtney took off in a sprint, half the girls were still staring slack jawed at the most handsome man they'd ever laid eyes on.

Four times around the field is a mile and Courtney ran as fast as she could. Chelsea Luzzato, who has always been considered the best runner in our class tried to catch her, but it was impossible. I fell in behind Clancy Penfield because she had math with me and I'd heard her say that she got stomach-aches whenever she ran too hard. We stayed in the middle of the pack, which meant that Courtney lapped us on our third time around.

Otto rewarded Courtney with a small smile but didn't even say anything about the fact that she'd just run the mile in five minutes and fifty-one seconds. But his smile was enough. She took her hair out of her ponytail and let it loose (which she never did) and waited patiently for his next instruction. I was shocked.

The next thing I knew he had us in two lines while he watched as we dribbled a ball through a long course of orange cones. Courtney didn't even check to see what line I was in. She went straight to the front of the first row and effortlessly worked her way around the obstacles at high speed. She was going to make it absolutely clear that no one could question who the best girl soccer player was.

I'd never seen her try so hard at anything. It was like watching a tornado take shape.

THIRTEEN

Before, my plan had been to just make it look like I cared. Now I was really, truly trying. But it didn't matter because even giving it my full effort I was horrible. Thanks to Courtney's daily sprints home I was now at least an average runner. But when we did the cone course it was obvious I had zero control of the soccer ball.

On my first touch I sent it flying way too far and when I went to get the ball, I tripped and fell. I got up off the ground like it was no big deal even though I was sure I'd actually broken my kneecap or at least fractured it. Small fractures are very hard to see on x-rays and even if they took me into the hospital it would be hard to know for sure. So I didn't say I wanted medical attention, even though I thought I should have, and I limped back to the end of the line and then let a bunch of girls cut in front of me while I tried to regain feeling in my leg.

On my second cone course attempt I went so slowly I

heard some of the girls snicker. I don't even blame them because I was really holding things up. I went to the bathroom
instead of doing the course a third time and I didn't come back
out onto the field until we were on the final trial of the day,
which was a series of drop kicks. Because I'd been fooled into
kicking the ball every day after school, I could at least boot the
thing part way across the field. Courtney of course, had the
hardest kick by far, sending the ball from midfield all the way
to the goal line. She apologized after her turn was up for not
really getting her foot underneath it right.

Our first day of try-outs ended with another lap around
the field and a series of stretches in a circle. Otto asked Courtney
to lead the stretching exercises. This was about the only thing
I was good at. Because I don't have any muscles I can pretty
much bend in any direction. It's kind of like watching a flex-
ible stick insect. I can really fold over.

Otto clapped his hands, thanked us all for coming and
said he'd see us tomorrow. He added that he thought we had a
lot of talent. He was looking at Courtney when he said it and I
could see her cheeks burn red and it had nothing to do with the
fact that she'd just run another record lap.

We all walked back to the gym in silence. And it wasn't
because we literally had the wind taken out of us. That's what
real greatness will do. It shuts you up.

Once we were in the warm confines of the girls' locker
room we all just sort of exploded. Helen Herlihy started giggling and couldn't stop. Katie Lopez instantly got the hiccups.
Rosie Chung started singing. Christine Blum jumped up on
the benches and did this gross dance she saw on MTV or some-

thing. Amy Maclellan took off most of her clothes and put them on her head. And Lauren Fenulli opened a huge bag of Doritos she had in her backpack and everyone began stuffing their faces, talking as they chewed. It was totally crazy.

Suddenly it didn't matter that I was Courtney's loser friend who could barely kick the ball. I'd been there. I'd witnessed the miracle. I was part of the group.

I was surprised at how good that felt.

After a while Coach Moshofsky came in and yelled at us really bad so we all calmed down.

Courtney and I walked home and for the first time in two months she didn't see anything scary in the shadows. It took us almost an hour to make it to her house and she talked about him the whole way.

When we said good-bye I meant it when I said I hoped I made the team but I really didn't think I had a chance since he was going to have to cut at least seven players and I was clearly one of the worst girls. Courtney stopped looking off into the distance and focused on me. It was as if everything else I'd said in the last hour was just noise. This she heard. When she spoke it was in a whisper:

"No. I want you to be there. I want you to be part of this."

I could tell she really meant it and I nodded back in a way she knew would mean I got that she still cared about me even if she now had a real reason to get up in the morning.

I ran the rest of the way home even though I was completely and totally tired because it was now night and I can't stand to be out in the dark by myself even if it's not yet six o'clock and there are people all around and lights on in the houses and the smell of different dinners cooking in the air. There were too many things I couldn't see.

When I got into the house Nammy was asleep in her chair and that was good because I thought she might be worried since I was so late. I got closer and saw her wallet was by the phone, which was bad. We'd be getting something delivered in a few days from some warehouse somewhere and who knows how we'd pay for it. If it was Saturday it was possible for me to get to the mail guy first and if it were C.O.D. I'd send the package back saying we didn't order the thing to begin with.

After I had some celery with peanut butter and a frozen waffle I took my soccer shoes out of my backpack. The bottoms were now coated with mud and grass. I put them on the steps outside because there are millions of bacteria and germs in fresh dirt. But later I couldn't sleep because I was worried about them, even though it's crazy to think someone would go into our backyard to steal a pair of girl's soccer shoes.

So I got up and brought them back in and cleaned off all the dirt with a steak knife and then I wrapped them in a bag and put them by the front door. And then I fell asleep and it was a thick kind of sleep where it's like someone's frozen you solid and when you wake up you don't even know where you are because it's so different from what was going on in your sleeping head. That's how far away I was.

And then I remembered where I'd been in my dream. I was on a big green field running in the full sun. And I was kicking a soccer ball.

54

FOURTEEN

For the next two days we continued to practice. Even someone like me who doesn't know anything about sports could figure it all out. We broke down into four groups. The first was the Stars. This was Courtney and her smaller Stars, Drina Archer and Helen Herlihy. The Stars were always at the right place at the right time. Their bodies moved in ways that made you stand up and take notice. They had some inner feeling about the ball and what was going on and they saw the game in a way that the rest of us never could. They were the bright spots in the field.

Behind the Stars were the Strong Players. There was a group of three of them, led by Rosie Chung who was left-handed and left-footed and just all around doing good stuff on the left side of life. The Strong Players were good athletes and played other sports and probably walked early as babies.

After the Strong Players were the Players. This group

was the largest and had the girls who at least knew what they were doing and were pretty good at sports and probably all had Dads who watched ESPN with them or something. The Players had good days and bad days and things they could do and things they couldn't but they always knew what was going on. After the Players there was a group of Losers.

I think it's important to say that I was not the loser of the Losers. I would have been for sure if I hadn't been running and kicking with Courtney before this all started. The Losers had all kinds of reasons for being there. Two girls each had a big sister who was a good player and even though they didn't have any talent or interest they were just expected to play. Three of the loser girls had just shown up looking for something to do. They were open-faced, and without worry or fear. They were no good at soccer but it didn't seem to matter. Their attitude was that they were up for some fun and if it didn't work out there was always something else to do and who really cared about any of it anyway?

That wasn't the attitude of the last four Losers. They were strugglers. They tried and tried hard, but their bodies didn't cooperate. When they kicked the ball they often missed and got the air. When they ran their legs would twist up, or cramp, or wear out. They got side aches and shin splints and headaches. They were always thirsty and tired and sweaty.

I was a Loser who knew I was a Loser, which wasn't true of all of us. Every now and then there is a Loser who thinks they are really a Player, or even worse, a Loser who thinks she's a Strong Player. Anyone who is jumping two whole categories is really out of touch with the real world. This is a

Super Loser. Your heart has to go out to them. But it doesn't. Instead you just wanted to scream because they should have been wearing signs on their backs saying, "Cut Me. I deserve it."

Otto pretended he couldn't figure all of this out in ten minutes when I know he did. Instead he made notes on his clipboard and shouted encouraging things now and then, and instructions like "go to the ball" and "put your body into it." He wore a green sweatshirt on the second day with yellow writing in what must have been Hungarian and then the faded blue one from the first day on the last day. When I wasn't sweating or cramping or hanging my head dry-mouthed, I was, like the rest of the girls, watching him.

He only got better. On the second day he put his clipboard down and came out on the field to actually show us how to kick since most of us were doing it wrong. He asked us to get in close, which was like throwing out bread for the seagulls at the dump. We were right next to him in a flash. He then had to tell us to step back because he probably couldn't even breathe.

On the third day Otto came out on the field and played with us. He picked out Courtney and her two minor Stars as one team and they took the whole rest of us on. Even though there were only four of them they scored three goals before the rest of us knew what was even going on. I think he did it because he wanted to get out there and see how good the Stars really were, not to show off or make us feel bad because after five minutes he put an end to the whole experiment.

But during those five minutes Courtney never looked so happy. They'd run down the field passing back and forth while the rest of us stood with our mouths open just trying to keep from being mowed down. Otto could do anything with a soccer ball. Just watching his feet made me dizzy.

When I wasn't at practice I couldn't help but think about him. It was like I had a can of soda open inside my stomach and it was him and it was just constantly releasing these "Otto bubbles," which would float right up through my body and then pop at the top of my head with a fizzle. It left me feeling achy and kind of confused and made it harder to breathe and eat my celery sticks with peanut butter.

At the end of our last day of tryouts he gave a speech thanking all of us for our efforts and saying how sorry he was that we couldn't just have a team with twenty-seven girls. He really looked sad about it, although I can't imagine why because the Losers were really starting to get on everyone's nerves and the Super Loser was in danger of being assaulted.

A list was going to be posted in the morning on the door of the gym. He wished us all good luck and told us to keep kicking balls, which made it hard not to laugh. We all turned to the gym in the low light and walked back knowing that we'd just had three of the most important days of our lives.

All of us except Courtney. She waited until the last girl was a good twenty yards away and then I saw her go to Otto. She said something to him that no one could hear. I saw his face. He was surprised. He said something back and she shook her head and then abruptly turned and started off in a jog after the rest of us.

But I kept my eyes on Otto which wasn't hard to do because he was now staring at me.

58

FIFTEEN

Courtney called her father from a payphone in the gym because she said she didn't want to walk home but I think it was because she didn't feel like talking. With the swarm of other girls in the locker room I couldn't ask her why she stayed behind to say something to Otto and she didn't volunteer anything. She was just real quiet and looked sort of defeated.

Mr. Bilsesser arrived right away in their Volvo station wagon and made us listen to a song about bacon cheeseburgers, which was so stupid you couldn't even believe it. We told him it was real cool and then he got all happy and played it five more times. By the time they dropped me off I'd made the decision to never eat another bacon cheeseburger as long as I lived, especially if it was from the place Mr. Bilsesser was advertising.

Inside our house Nammy was doing a crossword puzzle. She had a clear plastic bag over her head and I could see heaps of purplish goop on her hair. This meant she was dying it but this didn't always work right. Even when the color was what she wanted she always missed big spots and ended up looking like a cheetah in the back.

Nammy knew I'd been trying out for soccer but she didn't have any experience with sports and only understood bowling which she'd done a lot when she was younger and her fourth husband Rayford had been in a league. She still had her turquoise colored shirt that had "Bay City Bowler" stitched in red on the back and 'Renata' in black on the sleeve. She didn't fit into it anymore. Nammy says people are just like old dogs. They all get thick in the middle and their heads hang lower and in the end most have eyes that look like someone spilled milk in them.

Nammy called out for me to bring her an appetizer plate, which I'd been doing since I was a real little kid. I'd put pickles and olives and crackers on one of our fancy trays with a can of sardines on the side. That's where I draw the line. I won't open the sardine tin. Just the smell of those oily little fish makes me sick. I got a new Diet Coke and brought it along, too, with a lot of ice. She smiled big when she saw it all. I told her to keep her eye on the clock but I could tell she wasn't listening because she was all over the pickles and crackers.

After my bath and my celery and peanut butter I went to my room and cleaned my soccer shoes for the last time. I still had the box they came in. I wrapped them up in the tissue and then put them all the way in the back of my closet next to the big trunk I have of my Mom's stuff. I was trying as hard as I could not to open the trunk because I made a promise to myself that I wouldn't do it so much. There are only so many times you can look through the same dresses and shoes and shirts and stuff.

But I couldn't help myself. I opened the trunk and got out my Mom's old blue raincoat and her yearbook from high school. I'd looked at every page so many times I'd memorized it all but it didn't matter. I put on the raincoat, which was way too big for me. I always think I can still smell her when I have on that coat but I'm pretty sure I'm imagining it because it's been so many years now. I think the coat just smells like me and that means it smells like the bubble bath which is really the dishwashing soap and the smell of the stuff I put on my lips so they don't get all dry and crackly.

After about an hour of going through the yearbook I went out to get a glass a water and realized that Nammy was still in her chair and the plastic goop bag was still on her head. The appetizer tray was on her lap and all the pickles were gone and most of the olives and only two sardines were left in the oily tin. She'd fallen asleep. She must have had that purple goop on for over three hours and it was all bubbly inside the plastic and I couldn't even see her hair anymore.

I woke her up and helped her into the bathroom. Nammy got into the tub because she doesn't like showers at all even though they would be so much easier for her I can't believe it. She has a pot from the kitchen next to the tub and she uses it to pour water over her head. When she did all the goop came off and so did most of her hair. I guess the chemicals cooked it or something. Her hair in the back must be stronger because part of it stayed in so she had a ring of really weird yellow hair like a clown. She was not happy.

After she dried off and put on her sweat pants and a

shirt with little elephants on it, she tried on a lot of hats but they all looked bad. So I forced myself to be as brave as I could and I went up to the attic (which is a natural home for spiders and other very, very scary things). I found a box with old Halloween costumes and even though I was tempted to pull out an old clown one I took a wig instead. It had long, straight black hair and I think was from a really bad 'Sonny and Cher' dress-up set from years ago. Nammy put it on and looked about a hundred times weirder but not in her mind. She liked it.

When I finally went to bed it was really late and I knew I'd be so tired the next day I'd feel sick because that's what happens to me when I don't get enough sleep. I feel like I'm going to throw up. Nammy came into my room in the crazy long wig and kissed me goodnight like I was a little kid, which she never does anymore.

She stood in the doorway and sang for awhile:

"I got you, Babe."

SIXTEEN

The next day I was so exhausted I could barely get going in the morning. I even put two extra teaspoons of instant coffee in my cup but it didn't help. It only made it taste really gross.

When I got to school I was late and went straight to homeroom. Mrs. Wiener was giving us our morning announcements and telling us about some big problem the school was having with kids stealing rolls of toilet paper which I found hard to believe because the toilet paper they have here comes in cylinders the size of a tire and was made by convicts or something. It's so tough you almost need a knife to get a piece off. The problem with Mrs. Wiener was that she got everything mixed up all the time.

Courtney was in her seat smiling which isn't that weird because she does that a lot. I sat down next to her and was going to tell her about Nammy's hair falling out but I didn't have a chance because she just blurted out:

"Did you go look to see who made the soccer team?"

I thought she was being a show-off, which isn't like her at all.

"Like you ever thought you wouldn't?"

She rolled her eyes.

"You should look at the list."

Maybe there was some kind of joke on it or maybe some surprise about Otto. Whatever it was made her all giggly. I knew the list was supposed to be posted on the door of the gym but I'd been late and besides it was just something to make me feel bad so on purpose I'd entered the side door to avoid it. Now I was rolling my eyes.

"Just tell me."

But she wouldn't. That made me mad. So I pretended to listen to Mrs. Wiener and even scribbled a note to do a little investigation into the toilet paper problem. Courtney kept smiling and didn't seem to mind.

Once the bell rang and we got out into the hallway she grabbed my sleeve.

"Come on. We'll go look."

I went along because what else was I supposed to do? Courtney was moving fast now and we bumped into a few people who only smiled at her like it was no big deal and glared at me like I'd just given them a bleeding bruise.

When we got to the gym there were a few girls standing by the door. They moved out of the way at the sight of Courtney because she's, well, Courtney and most people step back when they see her just out of respect. The only other time

I'd seen a list like this it came from a computer and was printed up in alphabetical order. This one wasn't. It was written in blue pen in a kind of formal handwriting I hadn't seen before where the capitals have more curves or something and look fancy.

The first thing I saw was my name. I just stared. Courtney was just about to explode at this point.

"Well? What do you think?!"

I couldn't even speak. I looked again because what was my name doing up there?

Courtney put her hand on my shoulder and spun me around.

"You made the team! Can you believe it?"

Obviously I couldn't. I looked back at the piece of paper.

"It must be wrong."

Courtney couldn't take it anymore. She was insistent now.

"You're on the team. You made the cut. We're going to play soccer."

I turned and in one quick move flew right past her and into the girls' bathroom across the hall. I went for the first open stall door and when I pushed, it slammed straight into Marla Gaiser who had just unlocked it to come out. I bounced backwards and went into the next stall without even apologizing. Just after I turned the lock on the door I heard, "Sasha! What's going on?"

It was Courtney and she sounded upset. I didn't answer. In the hallway the bell rang, echoing in the tiled room and I could hear the other girls leave for class.

But not Courtney. She bent down and must have seen my feet because the next thing I knew she was in the stall next door standing up on the toilet peering over the divider at me.

"What's wrong?"

I looked up at her and when I did my eyes were suddenly all watery and my nose felt tight like the air in it went straight down into my lungs in a weird and maybe even dangerous way. Speaking was going to be a problem. She continued:

"Aren't you happy?"

I nodded my head and was able to murmur:

"Yeah."

She looked confused.

"Then why are you hiding in the bathroom?"

My ears were burning now, too, like someone stuck a match on the bottom of my lobes and the flames were leaping upwards. I managed to say:

"Because I'm afraid it will go away."

She answered "What will go away?"

I finally answered, "The feeling. The feeling of being really happy."

Courtney's brow knitted. If she wasn't careful she was going to have all kinds of bad lines in her forehead when she was older.

"You're crazy."

I felt pretty sure I wasn't going to cry so I said:

"You just now figured that out?"

That made her smile. I think she had a lot invested in

my being about a hundred times more normal than I actually am. I continued:

"You better get going or you'll be late to math."

That got her. Math was one of her favorite subjects. She jumped down off the toilet seat and ran from the room, calling over her shoulder:

"Congratulations, you nut!"

When I was sure she was gone I put my head in my hands. My ears weren't really on fire and my breathing was returning to normal. Obviously I couldn't explain to someone like her that once someone like me starts crying it could go on for days or even weeks. The secret was to just never start no matter what.

My nose was still sort of running and I bent over to get a piece of the butcher paper they call toilet paper and nothing was in the huge roller. For the first time all morning I smiled. Mrs. Wiener was right for a change.

SEVENTEEN

I got to science class late and had to make up an excuse about getting a nose bleed which worked because my nose was real red and I did really look like I'd just been through some kind of real trauma. Ms. Biculos was taking us into the library to do research for the dreaded science fair and I was lucky because I almost missed the whole thing.

Instead of looking for books about mold and doing my mandatory forty-five fact based index cards, I pretended to work while I was really trying to lower my blood pressure and stop freaking out about the whole soccer thing. Obviously Courtney had cut some kind of deal with Otto. There's no way I deserved to be on the team. What was she thinking?

I immediately started picturing all the ways I could die on a soccer field. It seemed pretty obvious to me that if I ran into one of the goal posts the head injury alone would kill me. If I didn't just croak on the field, I'd end up in a group home making things out of Popsicle sticks all day. Most people probably don't worry about running full speed into a goal post, but they don't play my style of the game.

After I got tired of worrying about that, I moved on to all the other possible problems I would face as a soccer player. Being kicked is not my idea of a good time. I know for a fact that the things that are supposed to protect your shins should be made out of metal. And why weren't players forced to wear padding and a helmet? If you're a kid it's against the law to even ride your bike without protective headgear. You can't play t-ball when you're tiny unless you have on one of those big plastic hats. Obviously someone hasn't been paying attention. I decided I would make it my crusade to change the sport. I'd try to convince our team, and then all the teams in the league, to wear thick padded pants, football helmets, and elbow and wrist guards for the horrendous falls. My final and most brilliant addition to the game would be the introduction of soft tipped shoes; designed to lessen the blow a player felt when another player kicked him or her.

I realized that my new soft-tipped soccer shoes might be hard to kick the ball with, but I think safety concerns should always be the first thing athletes and their fans think of. That's why if I were in charge of the world diving championships my inaugural move would be to get rid of the high board. There is no reason on earth anyone needs to jump, much less dive, off something that far off the ground.

I wrote all my new soccer plans carefully down on my science index cards, and Mrs. Biculos, who is always about half out of her mind, passed by my little cubby and whispered what a great job I was doing. I smiled big and told her how I was really enjoying the assignment. It's amazing how much of this science class is telling the person in charge what she wants to hear. Probably the rest of life is too but at this point I don't know about any of that.

After I'd filled about fifteen cards with my soccer safety ideas I was feeling sort of normal. I had eleven minutes more of research time left so I went and got my favorite book which is called "Anomalies of Nature." I am certain that the school has no idea that this book is part of their collection. I discovered it last year when I was on a mission to find the oldest book in the library. It turns out I later found an older one on covered wagons but I'd never come upon anything this good and I knew it right away.

"Anomalies of Nature" is really, really old. The pages have turned the color of putty and are crisp and hard on the edges. But the photographs are what this book is all about. It's basically a freak show. There are pictures of Siamese twins, a snake with two heads, and a woman with a full beard and moustache. And that's just for starters. There is a cow with five legs, a frog with part of his brain on the outside, and a man with a foot the size of a suitcase. The foot is all covered in spots and scales. You just can't take your eyes off it.

I've always wanted to check the book out and take it home, but I know if our librarian, Ms. Tartuffe, saw any of the pictures she'd take it away and then it would be gone for good. So I just have to read it when I can, which is about once a week. Even though the pictures are the best part, the stories of the people are great, too. The woman with the beard and the moustache that goes all the way to the floor worked in a circus and married a man who was an acrobat. They had four boys and one of them was born with webbed feet. There isn't a picture of him, which I think is very unfair. I'm glad she found someone to marry and he let her live her own life and didn't pressure her to shave off the beard although I don't really know why she didn't because she would have looked a lot better.

When I search through the book I get sad. Not because of the strange stuff but because the book is so old I know that all the people in the pictures are now dead. It's a weird feeling. Kind of like watching a black and white movie on cable TV and enjoying it and then thinking none of the people are even around anymore. It makes you suddenly feel real lonely.

My favorite person in the book is a tiny man named Leon Rildenstein. He's standing on a coffee table and there is a squirrel on his hind legs next to him. Leon isn't very much bigger than the squirrel. They are both holding nuts.

When I look at the picture I can tell Leon Rildenstein is afraid of the squirrel. I understand. If there were a squirrel my size looking at me with his sharp claws and pointy teeth, I'd be afraid, too.

EIGHTEEN

For the rest of the day I tried not to obsessively think about soccer even though I told my friend Jose that I made the team. He was really happy because in his country soccer is the national sport and everyone plays. He said he'd give me all kinds of pointers but he didn't use the word 'pointers' because he doesn't know that word but I'm sure that's what he meant. Jose's now studying to be an ambulance driver. He only needs to finish one more course and he'll be ready. I feel good that someone like Jose will be out there driving around in case I need to go to the hospital. I know he'll drive fast and still make sure I'm breathing.

After our last class of the day I met Courtney at our lockers which are of course, right next to each other. She couldn't believe I didn't bring my soccer shoes to school even though I tried to explain to her that since I never thought I'd make the team I hadn't planned on ever wearing them again. We went to the gym and when we passed by Coach Moshofsky's office she gave Courtney a weird look. Courtney said I was crazy but I wasn't because I saw the way she looked at her and it was one of those sly looks that says you've done something wrong. Courtney doesn't do very much that's wrong so she doesn't know the look. I do.

After we put on our PE clothes we went outside. All the Losers except me were gone, and of course so was the Super Loser. The team now was just the Stars and the Strong Players and most of the Players. Everyone looked sort of surprised to see me even though you'd think they could all read and saw the list. Courtney stayed right at my side like a guard dog or something and so no one said anything.

When we got out onto the field Otto was waiting. He had all kinds of paperwork for us. There was a schedule of games and a release form for our parents to sign that said no matter what kind of injury happened to us during the season we couldn't blame the school because it was all our fault.

After we put the papers down and ran four times around the field, Otto wanted to talk to us about what position we each were interested in playing. I figured my position would be on the bench. But he wanted to know if we saw ourselves as offensive players or defensive. Courtney whispered to me to say 'defense,' which I did. I thought he'd then split us up into groups but it wasn't like doing a history project. We just stayed together and did all kinds of drills including running back and forth fast across the field touching the ground at the end, which he called "wind sprints." They were designed to kill you.

I could pretty much keep up with the other players even though I was the only one who had on regular shoes and didn't have legs with muscles you could see. I weigh a lot less than the other girls and while we were catching our breath from running around like a pack of pound dogs, Otto gave us a talk about nutrition. He said it was really important that we eat right. Breakfast is really a big deal to him. I didn't volunteer that I always have instant coffee and then a plate of small marshmallows. He said that we needed to drink water all day and eat carbohydrates before we had big games. He said we should eat what our parents make us because they know good food from junk food. He told us to eat a lot of green vegetables.

Obviously he doesn't know about my Nammy. I can't even remember the last time she made a meal for me and her idea of green vegetables is hot dog relish, which I don't even like. I was hoping that celery was a big deal to him but he didn't bring it up.

After the food talk he said a bunch of stuff about being a team and sticking together and using each other's talents because we were all there for a reason and we each had something special to offer. I caught a couple girls looking at me weird but I just ignored it because I'm used to that kind of thing.

It was starting to get dark when he said we were done. I was so tired I couldn't believe it. My hair was all sweaty and my face was red and I could tell I was getting a rash on my back. Courtney didn't even look like she'd done anything. She spent the whole practice watching Otto and listening to him as if there was some kind of secret message in everything he said and she only had a few minutes to figure it out or we'd all be blown up. We turned back to the gym when Otto called my name.

"Sasha, can I speak to you?"

It was the moment I'd been waiting for. He was going to tell me that somehow he'd mixed me up with one of the other girls and written down the wrong name and now he was hoping I understood that he was a foreigner and didn't mean anything by it. I just looked at him waiting for the speech.

"You're new to soccer."

I nodded my head.

"I think you have a lot of potential."

When someone tells you that you have a lot of potential it means you're really bad.

I nodded again.

"I've been thinking about the team and I figure goalie might be a good place for you."

The way he said this made me feel like I was a piece of furniture someone made him take that he hated and he just realized he could put it in the garage. I just stared at him. I may not know anything about the game but I do know that being the goalie is the scariest thing you can do on a soccer field. Balls are kicked at incredible speeds and you are supposed to on purpose throw yourself in front of them. My whole body went stiff.

"Madeline Bingham is our goalie."

Now he was nodding.

"You're right. But we'll need a back-up."

I just looked at him blankly as I said, "I think Shawna Sully wants to be the back-up."

He nodded again.

"Yes. But we'll need a back-up to the back-up."

A back-up to a back-up. It was perfect. I wouldn't get near the ball in a real game. I smiled:

"It sounds good."

And I meant it. He was smiling now, too. His smile was all white teeth and for a second I felt like if he told me to run out onto the highway and stop traffic I'd do it.

He winked at me as he said, "It's settled then."

NINETEEN

We practiced every day after school for the first week and by Friday I had blisters all over my feet and was limping. I couldn't believe how much we had to run. First around the field. Then across it a million times. We ran diagonally and in circles. We stomped on every blade of grass until it all looked as flat and worn as an old green rug.

I was now exhausted all the time. And hungry. Mostly I never have much of an appetite. Nammy has always called me the world's pickiest eater because I'd rather have little pains in my stomach than swallow something that I think smells weird. But after a few soccer practices I added a piece of toast in the morning to my instant coffee and marshmallows. And I started eating lunch. Normally I'd just go to the cafeteria with Courtney and sit with her while she ate the peanut butter sandwich her dad had packed in a brown bag. I sometimes had a few of her chips. And even though I'd always qualified for a free hot lunch card, I never even bothered going to the office to pick it up. Now I did.

A lot of things in the hot lunch line freak me out. Every day there was mystery meat, which was always swimming in a thick gray sauce and smelled like the dead leaves on the street that pile up in the gutter. I couldn't even look at it. In the tray next to the 'MM' was rice or noodles, and the next pan always has some kind of potato dish. This is followed by a big section of steamed vegetables and I swear they just put out the same ones every day because I've never seen one kid take any. After the display-only broccoli and carrots, the few things I would consider swallowing began. There is Jell-O. Canned fruit. Cottage cheese. And then bread products.

A typical meal once I began soccer was a canned peach with three packages of saltine crackers and a little container of peanuts. Courtney was real happy that after all these years I was eating something during the day. She said it was a start.

Having Nammy as my "parents" has probably affected me a lot in the food department. She eats the grossest things. Her favorite meal is pickled herring in sour cream. It looks like snakes in a jar. She also loves really smelly cheese and anything with hot sauce or clumps of garlic. She puts all kinds of things together that weren't meant to be paired, like scrambled eggs and tuna fish fried with a can of chili. Nammy will pretty much eat anything. I can prove it.

A couple of Christmases ago the Pinkstons who live down the street from us had a holiday party. I think they were feeling all generous or something because they invited me and Nammy. I didn't want to go but Nammy said it would be good for us to get out of the house and she can't resist a buffet table. So she put on this pair of bright orange pants that make her look like a highway worker and then a sweater she loves with flying reindeer. She hadn't eaten very much all day because she was thinking about all the stuff the Pinkstons would have and saving up to pig out there.

We got to their house late because she could only find one of her gold boots and we looked for about an hour for the other one and then finally gave up. It was really crowded by the front door when we walked up and Nammy saw this neighbor she doesn't like named Mr. Serenbri. He once told her we didn't bag our garbage right and that's why the neighborhood had rodent problems. So Nammy said we had to go around and enter through the back door which I wasn't crazy about but she was the adult and I was only the kid. We made our way around the side of the house through these thick shrubs which kept whipping into my face because Nammy was going first and acting like she knew what she was doing by leading the way.

We finally got to the back of the house and of course no one was out there but you could see the party going on inside. There was a picnic table and chairs in the yard but no decorations or anything. On top of the picnic table were two small bowls and Nammy reached in and scooped up a handful of the crunchy stuff inside. She offered it to me but I don't like party mix so of course I said no. She ate the little red stars and then complained that they tasted real fishy and were dry and salty. So she scooped up another handful and this time she dipped them into the second bowl which had cottage cheese. She kept chewing. She said the party mix wasn't very good and she hoped it wasn't any kind of warning about the rest of the Pinkston's spread.

We came in the back door into the kitchen, which surprised everyone and Nammy went straight for a big platter of Swedish meatballs which had cute little toothpicks with plastic Santa heads stuck in them. I went to sit in a chair along the wall because I didn't really know anyone and most of the people had been drinking the eggnog with rum for hours and now had red noses and were talking too loud. I was really bored and was staring out the window into the yard and I suddenly saw two cats jump up onto the picnic table and start eating out of the bowls of party mix and dip. I didn't think this was right so I went into the kitchen and found Mrs. Pinkston and told her that there were cats outside getting the appetizers. She opened her big-red-lipstick-ringed mouth and laughed and said they were only eating their cat food. The little darlings get cottage cheese with their kibble. I watched Nammy real close all night and she never got sick or anything so I didn't tell her.

We didn't get asked back the next year and Nammy was real sad and mopey when she saw all the holiday lights on and people heading down to their house all dressed up and laughing. She talked about the Swedish meatballs for about an hour and I couldn't take it anymore so I told her about the cat food to make her feel better. Nammy got a stomach ache right away that night even though it had been a year. She was in bed for the week and even got a fever. That's when I knew for sure that food is a powerful and strange thing. And unfortunately most of what you think about it is in your head.

TWENTY

After two weeks of Otto's conditioning we were ready to pay attention to the game. Courtney was our center midfielder and on special occasions would go up and play forward. The other girls were sprinkled around the field depending on whether they had speed or a good kick or some skill I didn't know about. I still didn't really understand the game even though it wasn't that complicated. You want to kick the ball into the other side's net. When you do everyone cheers and you get a point. When they kick it into your net everyone gets mad and they get the point. There aren't different points for doing the same thing different ways like in football or even basketball. And even though you can do good things on your own, you need the rest of the players to make any of it work so it's really a team sport which is kind of nice.

Once we started playing practice games Madeline Bingham was one goalie and Shawna Sully took the other side.

That left me to chase after balls and generally hang out near Otto. Madeline and Shawna did their best to include me when we did our separate goalie drills, but I really didn't like anyone to take a shot on the goal if I was in front of it, so my practice was kind of limited.

Madeline was a natural goalie. She's tall and strong and can kick the ball further than anyone on our team except Courtney. Madeline's big brother plays soccer and is some kind of star and is on a club team and drives all over the place on weekends going to games. Madeline told me she never wanted to be a goalie but the AYSO coach she had when she was little made her because she was taller than the other girls and he thought she'd be able to reach farther to stop balls. After she'd done it for a season they just expected her to do it again and then everyone just thought of her as a goalie and she couldn't get out of it after that.

I think that's why it's important in life not to go to dental school unless you really want to be a dentist, because once people see you training at something they just get it in their heads that's what you do. But how are you supposed to know you'd want to be a dentist until you've tried? That's where the problem is in a lot of things that grown-ups have to face. You could start doing something and maybe you don't even care about it and then you realize a ton of time later you got trapped into doing it for life. That's why I will never, ever work in a funeral parlor. I know I'd get stuck there forever.

Even though Madeline doesn't like being a goalie she's really great at being a goalie. She watches the field and moves around constantly like a shark guarding a cave or something.

And when the ball comes toward her she starts yelling to her players and telling them where to go. She says she can see the game in a way no one else can but the other goalie because it's all happening right in front of her like the field's a stage and she's the audience.

The other reason Madeline is so good is because she's not afraid. She just wants the ball to hit her. She'll dive straight out like she's going to land in water but she doesn't. She hits the dirt hard and never cries or even complains, which makes me wonder all the time what's wrong with her. She's real tough like a boy, which is funny because when she's not on the field she only talks about going shopping for new clothes and lip gloss. That's one of the things I like about the team. It's full of surprises.

Shawna Sully, who is our back-up goalie, is one of them. Shawna is good, but just not as good as Madeline because I don't think she's been doing it as long and she gets nervous and sort of falls apart. At first I thought there was something wrong with her eyes because Otto yelled to her all the time to 'focus' but he meant really for her to concentrate. Shawna is always thinking of about ten things at the same time and you could tell sometimes when she's on the field. She'll be look-ing one way which is where the ball is and then all of a sudden she'll just hear something or see something and she won't know what's going on. I try to be as encouraging as I can to her because I really think that it's brave to go for the job when you aren't just naturally talented like Madeline.

The good news for me is that I have them both there to play so everyone knows I really don't need to worry about ever taking the field. But I still feel like part of the team because I run the laps and chase the balls and Otto says I'm good at seeing little things so I watch for him to see if Nicole Parada is turning her foot out right like he said or if Helen Herlihy is going off-sides when no one's watching. She can't help herself. She gets excited and because she runs so fast she just goes right by the defender.

My life had a new routine now where I stayed after school to practice and then got picked up by Mr. Bilsesser and driven home. He usually had some kind of treat in the car for us, which was good, and he always asked a lot of boring questions, which was bad. Everyone thought our team was going to really go far this year because they said we had a lot of talent. They didn't mean me of course, but I'm always still happy to hear them say that. Eleanor Roosevelt's mascot is the Eagle. I don't know why because I don't think Eleanor Roosevelt as a person had anything to do with eagles but maybe it's because she liked them a lot or something.

So we were the Eagles and for the first time in my life since 'Campfire Girls' which is little Girl Scouts, I was a part of a group. I quit 'Campfire Girls' after only three weeks because Nammy didn't think it was a good thing to learn about starting fires even though I told her a bunch of times that wasn't part of it. But I was okay with quitting because I was afraid in the big, dark auditorium, which was where we had to meet and nobody was interested when I said we should find a new headquarters.

That's one good thing about a soccer field. I didn't have to worry about anyone sneaking up on me.

TWENTY-ONE

Our first game was on a Friday. We'd gotten our uniforms the day before and Coach asked us to wear them to school, which was weird for me because I've never done anything like that before and I swear it felt like the whole school was staring at me. Courtney's worn all kinds of uniforms and didn't think a thing about it. I tried on my shorts and shirt the night I got them and Nammy said I looked like a grasshopper. I think she said that because I have long, thin legs and I was squatting down.

Since I'm technically a goalie I don't just have a jersey, I also have a long sleeve shirt, but I put that away in my locker. I think it's only right for Madeline to walk around in that goalie shirt because she's the one really doing the job. When Otto handed out the uniforms I thought it was a good time to give my speech about maybe wearing helmets or other protective gear, but everyone just laughed like I was making a big joke so I had to pretend that I was. I think Otto was the only one who could tell I was serious because he looked at me real strange afterwards.

Everyone still thinks Otto's the hottest guy they've ever seen but we've gotten used to him now so it's not such a big deal. We've seen him burp and blow his nose and stick his finger in his ear and poke around for earwax. Plus we've all talked to him a lot so he's become about half human. Don't get me wrong, we still feel sort of light-headed when we first see him, but at least all of us can now breathe when we do.

I remember in second grade this new girl came to our school named Hilly Saunders. She had a big purplish patch on her face the size of a muffin, which was some kind of birthmark. When I first saw her I couldn't believe how strange she looked. A few of the mean boys nicknamed her 'Inky' because it looked like someone spilled ink on her and it never got cleaned up. When I talked to Hilly I had trouble because I wasn't sure if I should look at the purple spot or not look at the purple spot. I ended up mostly looking right past her left ear, which was as far away from the purple spot as my eyes could get. But then after awhile I just saw her every day and I guess I got used to it because after a while she didn't look weird anymore. And it wasn't just me. The mean boys stopped calling her 'Inky.' She was just Hilly who was good at kickball and had four hamsters. I guess it's kind of like Robbie Ellis having those really big ears. After awhile, who even notices?

So it was kind of that way with Otto, only in reverse. We all still knew he was incredible looking, and if the sun was going down and he was standing in front of it so that his head of curls were kind of glowing, it still felt like a spiritual experience or something. But otherwise he was the guy with the clipboard telling us to try harder. It's funny how doing things in a group can make you do way more than you'd do on your own. I would never in a million, trillion years go run around our field twelve times, (which is three miles). But by the time our first game arrived we'd been doing it a lot. In the beginning I got side aches and even was dizzy and thought my legs were going to fall off. After awhile I knew I'd live and then it just got sort of boring.

When we ran out of the gym to the field there were already parents and a bunch of kids hanging around waiting for the game. Courtney's Mom couldn't get away from work but her dad came and he brought juice boxes and protein bars and was all excited. He came over and told me he knew I'd do great. I smiled and didn't tell him I would never be part of the game, which was just the way I wanted it.

The team we played was from across town and came in an old orange bus with a gray front fender. The girls got off in their red uniforms and looked around like they couldn't believe what a dump our school was, which was insulting considering their bus didn't look so hot. Courtney knew some of the girls from all the other sports she's played and said they were a little stuck up but probably not dirty players or anything. I didn't even know what a dirty player was until their number six took the field and used her elbow as a weapon. She also held onto jerseys when she thought the referee wasn't looking and she pretended to trip all the time in order to go flying into one of our players and send them to the ground with her.

I'd never seen anything like it. All of the sudden the game looked even more violent and dangerous. From the safety of Otto's side I watched with my mouth open. I was stunned. Fortunately most of our team played as if it was no big deal. At half time we were ahead one to nothing when Helen Herlihy scored on Courtney's perfectly placed corner-kick. Otto made a bunch of adjustments during the break and when our team went back on the field we were playing with another forward up front and fewer mid-fielders. Otto had assigned me to keep track of statistics so I had to write down anytime that anyone on our team took a shot on the goal, even if they missed. I also had to keep track of who made the assists, and when Madeline made a save and stopped a goal and a bunch of other stuff. It kept me really busy. It also made me realize what was going on. The other team played most of the game on the left side of the field and had two strong players who kind of were in charge of the game. We had Courtney, who was better than all of them, and then four other players who were as good as their two stars. In the second half it all caught up to them even with their number six practically biting our players. We pulled ahead four to zero.

Even though I didn't set foot onto the field during regulation play I couldn't believe how happy I was when the referee blew the whistle three short times and put his hand out in the direction of our side. We'd won. I ran out onto the field with Otto and the other substitute players and we all were jumping up and down and kind of making really shrieky noises which normally I would have hated.

It wasn't until then that I saw Nammy. She was sitting in a lawn chair on our side of the field down by the end in a pink and gold jumpsuit. She was wearing her black "Cher" wig, which she'd given a haircut. It was now shoulder length and didn't look half as loony as it did when I left the house in the morning.

When she saw me she got up onto her feet and started cheering like I'd won the Olympics.

You just have to love Nammy.

TWENTY-TWO

After that first match Nammy was a real fan. It was hard for her to get to games and she never got to one on time, but she put her heart and soul into the idea of soccer. She started watching the Spanish language channel to catch matches and even claimed to be following the league in Brazil, but I didn't really believe her. She just tossed out a few names like she knew what was going on and then she'd sit back and smile and show all her teeth.

And pretty soon everything she was wearing was in our colors. She ordered a gob of new athletic sweaters she saw on TV and even found an old felt St. Patrick's Day hat with an eagle on it from her second husband Kirby who was Irish and liked to sing late at night. She still had a ton of his things even though they'd been divorced forever and he only lived over in Junction City and could have come and got the stuff if he'd ever wanted it.

Kirby had an electric rock polisher that was still in our garage and it made such a racket when it was on you thought you were going to scream just listening to that thing rumble. When I was younger I'd bring rocks home and then load them up in the polisher and plug it in. The rocks would roll around in there for hours making the kind of noise a metal zipper in the dryer makes only about a million times worse. I always thought one of the rocks would turn out to have a diamond in it and then me and Nammy would be rich and she could order anything she wanted on TV and I could get the home security system with the moving cameras and the twenty-four hour surveillance that I always dreamed about.

But the closest I came was a rock I found in the dirt by Williams's bakery that was dark green when I had finished polishing it. For awhile I thought I had something but I got a book out of the public library and it turned out to be some kind of common ore that all the mountains are made of around here. I still felt it was special so I figured it was magic. I'd make wishes on the rock but I was careful always to wish on things that I couldn't check up on like starving kids who lived in tents suddenly finding peanut butter sandwiches and jelly beans on their pillows in the morning.

Once soccer season started I took the rock with me to school every game day. I didn't tell anyone because it would be one more thing they didn't understand, and also because magic is more powerful when no one knows.

With the help of the rock and Courtney we won our second game by a score of four to three and everyone was surprised because the team from Jefferson always was really good. Courtney made two of the four goals and already was leading the league in scoring. They kept track of our league on the internet so we could go into the library and find out all the statistics. I checked a few times a day even though I knew things couldn't change. I'm like that sometimes. If I've boiled an egg I have to go back and check about ten times to make sure I turned off the stove. I read in a book that this might mean that later I could go crazy but since I'm still a kid I'm hoping it just means I'm careful.

In the second game Alexandra Leon hurt herself. The referee decided to do a drop ball after he stopped play because Alexandra and this other girl with frizzy hair from Jefferson were pushing and shoving each other and needed to be yelled at. I think a drop ball is just a plain bad idea. And after what happened I know Alexandra thinks so, too. The ref made them stand facing each other and then he dropped the ball down in between them. Alexandra took a huge step forward and put her whole body into her kick. So did the girl with frizzy hair from Jefferson. Unfortunately they both missed the ball and ended up kicking each other right in the foot.

They had to carry Alexandra off the field. She couldn't stop crying. The girl with the frizzy hair walked off but she had her coach and her mother on either side of her. They took Alexandra to the hospital right away and she had a fracture in the top part of her foot. They put her in a cast, even though they said it really was for her comfort and not to stabilize the injury. I asked her about ten times to bring her x-rays with her to school so I could see, but she never did.

So Alexandra was out for the season. She was good

about it and we all signed her cast and a lot of the boys in our grade got interested in the sport once they realized our team must be playing hard if one of us could break a bone. After that a group of the cool boys came to all our games. They always traveled around in a pack and spent a lot of time jumping up on top of each other. They didn't stand around and plot and plan like the girls. They were always chasing each other and hitting and making noise. Even the ones who I knew for a fact had a brain in their heads, like Pierre Van Riesselburg and Steve Acker, got all nuts when they were in a group.

Having the boys at our games made it hard for some of the girls to concentrate. This made Otto really upset. He made a rule that we had to stand on the sidelines and look out at the game, not back behind us at the old wooden bleachers. If he caught us with our heads the wrong way we had to run an extra lap around the field after the game was over. Amber Rizzo didn't care and ended up running at least two times around after every match. She also put on fresh lip gloss at halftime which Otto didn't allow and she had her mother take in the sides of her uniform shorts to make them fit tighter.

I didn't have a problem with her even though the first time she saw Nammy in her lawn chair on the sidelines she went crazy laughing. Courtney took her by the arm and went off far enough away that I couldn't hear. I don't know what she told her but after that Amber only smiled when she was near me and even offered to give me a beauty makeover at her house on a Saturday if I ever wanted to try it.

I told her I was always really busy on weekends, which was a lie and that I lived with a registered beautician, which was true. Nammy was trained to do a lot of things she didn't end up doing. It's what made her so good at the crossword puzzles.

TWENTY-THREE

We won our third game and everyone started talking about the possibility of an undefeated season. The kids in art class painted big signs with Eagles kicking soccer balls with their clawed feet and the drill team did a dance for us at an assembly. All of a sudden it was like the whole school was behind the team. Of course we then went out and lost our next game. I felt it coming. We were playing Franklin Middle School. And Ashley Aiken was their Captain.

I hadn't seen much of Ashley since I'd started soccer. I got a ride home from practice from Mr. Bilsesser every day so I didn't even have to walk around the block to avoid passing her house anymore. But we'd all heard that this year the other good girls' middle school soccer team was Franklin. So I can't say I hadn't thought about her.

The way our league works we play every team twice. The team with the best record in the end is the champion. When we got on the bus to go to Franklin we were both in the same position. Neither one of us had ever lost a game.

Otto stood up in the front of the bus and gave us a talk about playing hard and focusing and not getting too excited, but we were all too excited to hear any of it. Everybody had been fighting about who got to sit by who on the way over except for me and Courtney because we knew we'd just sit with each other.

Amber Rizzo got really mad at Shawna Sully because Shawna said she'd sit with her but also told Drina Archer the same thing. Shawna didn't think it was a big deal to do that but Amber did and then Drina got really mad at Amber even though Amber was just mad at Shawna. Rosie Chung wasn't trying to get involved but she did when she got up and moved over to where Drina was sitting. Amber yelled at Rosie, which was really not right and then Madeline got mad at Amber because she's really good friends with Rosie and couldn't stand to see her upset. Pretty soon everyone had an idea about who was to blame and by the time we got off the bus half of the girls weren't even speaking to the other half of the team.

That's not a good way to start a big game. We tried to patch things together when we were running around to warm up but that kind of problem doesn't go away with a few laps around a field and some kicks at the net. I think it was nerves that got the fight going to begin with.

Franklin Middle School is scary. Our school looks like a school. It's made of old brown bricks and has a ratty hedge growing around it that really is just a place for kids to litter. Franklin looks like a hospital or a factory or something. The

buildings are new and made of glass and metal, and everything looks sharp and like it could shatter and hurt you. That's
how it looked to me anyway. Instead of a set of old gray wooden
bleachers on the sidelines of the field they have shiny metal
seats and a real electric scoreboard with lights and everything.

Our soccer field is kind of lumpy with a few low places
where the water collects and slugs and bugs breed. There's a
group of gopher holes in the south corner, which can really get
you if you're not careful. Their field was perfectly flat and the
grass all grew evenly, not in different patches mixed up with
weeds like ours.

While we were warming up we acted like it was no big
deal but we were all impressed. The only thing we had that got
their attention was Otto. When Franklin's team ran out to the
field we were just getting off the bus and I saw the way the
girls looked at him. They were all talking and laughing and
having a good time until they saw our secret weapon and then
they all shut up right away and just stared. Their coach was a
woman who must have been in the army before she took the
job at Franklin. She barked orders so loud the veins in her neck
got all puffy and her face turned real red. And she didn't look
at Otto even once which is just wrong.

Ashley and I saw each other right away, and of course
she laughed. I know the idea of me playing a sport is amusing
but I don't think she handled it well. She laughed hard through
her nose and then pointed me out to a few of her teammates. I
just looked away because they were on the other half of the
field and I didn't want to cause trouble. I told Courtney about
it and she didn't say anything, she just nodded in a way that

said she got it.

Courtney plays 'center-mid,' which is short for the center mid-fielder. This is the player in the middle of the field who really works to control the game because everything goes through them. They run the distance from their own goal all the way to the other team's goal, sometimes with every play. The person playing 'center-mid' has to have all the skills of the other positions, like speed and the ability to control the ball, and a big kick. But Otto says that true soccer players have another thing, which is that they can see the field while they are playing. At first I just thought he meant that they could really see the field, which all of us can do, even Tabby Duggan and she's had glasses since she was five. But that's not what he was talking about.

When you see the field playing soccer you see what's happening where the ball isn't. You know what's ahead. Not like the lady on the cable channel who can tell you for money where your husband went with his golf shoes and your life-savings, but like playing chess or something. You're thinking about where the ball could go and who could be there. And you're doing that while you're running down the field getting in position to do something about it.

Not many players can really see the field. It takes all kinds of experience and Otto says it requires this other thing that I guess either you're born with, or you're not.

All I know is that Nammy says I was born with a fever and a rash all over my body. It took forceps and a suction cup and half the medicine in the hospital to get me out of my mother.

I guess I've always been afraid of the unknown.

TWENTY-FOUR

So we started out moving slow and just never caught up. Ashley Aiken was their center-mid and she lined up across from Courtney and said something that made Courtney's face squeeze up. They scored in the first five minutes and after that we were playing catch-up for the rest of the game, always a goal behind until we ran out of time and they won four to three.

On the bus ride home Madeline cried because being the goalie she felt like it was all her fault. Amber and Drina and Shawna went and sat by her and you would never have believed that two hours before they were all fighting about who was sitting where. Courtney was completely silent on the way back. She'd scored two goals and should have felt good about that but it wasn't enough because we didn't win. She looked out the window the whole ride and I could tell from her face that she was still playing the game so I didn't say anything.

When the bus pulled into the parking lot of the school Otto stood up to say something before we got off. I thought he was going to tell us to not feel bad because we'd tried hard and everything. But he didn't. It was dark outside and the only light came from the greenish dials on the dashboard. The driver turned to Otto and I thought even he looked real sad. And then Otto started talking. He said we had to do better. He said we had to try harder. He said they beat us to the ball. They were tougher, mentally and physically. He said he was disappointed in us. And he was disappointed in himself.

I could hear my heart pounding in my chest when he finished. I knew that meant my blood pressure was really high, and all of a sudden I wondered if I was going to have a heart attack or a stroke and just croak on the bus. My face was burning hot by the time he'd finished and my hair was all sticky with sweat. I thought for sure I was going to throw up but I hadn't eaten since lunch and I think all the crackers and cheese had already moved into my intestines or I would have.

Courtney and I got off the bus and found our backpacks in the gym and she still wasn't talking so I just followed at her side doing what she did because she knows how to act in these situations and it was all new to me. We got in Mr. Bilsesser's car and he said right away that Courtney had played a great game but she acted like she couldn't hear him and looked out the window again.

That's when I realized she was what they call a 'true competitor.' All the other girls felt bad right after we lost and felt real crummy again after Otto gave his bus speech but I could see them all talking and laughing going to their cars and I heard Rosie Chung telling a joke outside the gym. They were already over it and thinking about what was for dinner and who to call on the phone at night. But not Courtney. When she lost it hurt deep inside. I wanted to say it was only a game and it didn't matter but I could see that she didn't feel that way.

When her dad pulled up in front of my house I turned back to say good-bye and could tell by the way her jaw looked that she was grinding her teeth. All of a sudden I got it. Courtney didn't really care that much about soccer. She didn't care about being first in the league or being the most valuable player or getting another trophy. She cared about Otto. And she felt she let him down.

When I got in the house I made a little plate of celery and peanut butter and heated up some frozen enchiladas that were in an orange box marked with purple writing for my Nammy. I sat in front of the TV with her but even though it looked like I was watching the weather channel I was just thinking about Courtney and trying to figure it out. I decided that sometimes you could want things and do things more for someone else than for yourself. She was playing so hard for a man from Hungary with curly hair and a clipboard and she probably didn't even know it. All of a sudden I could see why people fought wars and jumped out of airplanes and did all kinds of wacky stuff. They had something else, maybe a person, floating around in the front of their brains and that changed the way they saw the world.

I went into my room and got out Mom's old trunk, where along with her stuff, I also kept a little notebook where I recorded really, really, really important things that were only for me to see and not forget. I think I got in the habit of doing this because I don't have parents. Maybe if you have them you don't need to write down these kinds of things because they can just tell you. I took a blue pen and wrote down that it was possible to make yourself better for someone else. I then wrote alongside this that you could be faster and stronger, too. I wasn't sure if you could be braver but after I thought about it a while I decided it was possible.

The last time I'd written in the notebook was when I realized that all people are gray. They weren't all good, or all bad. They were in the middle. Who they were was all about different shades. Finding this out helped when strange things happened like the time the man at the end of the street got mad and yelled at me to get off the sidewalk even though it's owned by the city and not him. I found out later that a car hit his dog that morning so he was just outside yelling at everyone all day.

I tried to tell myself that even awful Ashley Aiken was gray and had something that was good about her, like maybe she once helped an old lady across the street in a wheelchair, but I really doubted it.

Her team was better than we were. At least they were that afternoon. I just hoped for Courtney's sake it wouldn't stay that way.

TWENTY-FIVE

After that first loss our practices were a lot harder. We ran more and stayed on the field longer and a few of the parents complained because they sat in the parking lot at the end of the day waiting in their steamy cars. But they didn't moan about it to Otto because they knew that would be a mistake.

We have a rule in our school that if a parent talks to a coach during a game their kid automatically can't play anymore. They made the rule because last year a father in the middle of a football game pushed Mr. Ansell, who is the coach, and knocked him over. Mr. Ansell ran a play instead of calling a time-out. When he fell backwards he landed on this big Gatorade container and he hurt his back and he couldn't get up or anything. After that they made the parents of athletes come to school at night and listen to a lady talk about what competition was really all about. I don't know what she said because it was only for the adults and of course Nammy didn't go, but I think the "no-talking-to-the-coach" is a good rule because you just can't have parents pushing people like that.

We were all excited for our next game and anxious to show Otto and the world how much we'd improved and how seriously we were now taking the whole thing. We were playing Lincoln and they'd won two games and lost two games so we were feeling pretty good before we started.

The thing about sports, which I didn't know before but found out that day, is that the big unknown is whether someone will get hurt. I don't mean some little problem like Chelsea Luzzato has. She's always complaining about her knee hurting or a stomach ache or something. I mean an injury. I'm always looking for ways you can hurt yourself but when I'm outside I usually concentrate on possible falling objects and slippery surfaces. I wasn't thinking someone in a uniform could attack you.

That's what happened to Madeline. She was playing goalie and we were already up by two. The other team was really frustrated, I guess. At least their number ten was. Amber missed a pass from Drina and they got a break-away and came charging down the field. Their number six, who was their best player, passed to number ten, who was big for her age and had thick legs like trees. Madeline came right out of the goalie box because the ball was too far in front of number ten and she was fearless that way. She dove out straight at the ball like she was going to land in a pool of water. Number ten didn't care. She flung her foot back and kicked as hard as she could into what would have been the ball but turned out to be Madeline's knee.

You could tell right away it was bad. Madeline cried out in pain like she'd been shot. She landed on the ground and her knees went right up to her chest in a ball of agony. I couldn't see her face because it was burrowing down into the grass and dirt. I took off from my place right next to Otto and started out onto the field but Coach grabbed me and pulled me right back onto the sidelines. Even he had to wait until the ref signaled he could come out to help.

Chelsea Luzzato's grandfather was there and he's a doctor so they let him go out after Otto looked up with a face that we all could see said Madeline was really messed up. Some of the boys ran back to the gym and got Mr. Ansell to get the stretcher they keep in the supply closet for the football team. They ran out with it and Madeline got loaded up and carried to the parking lot by Chelsea's grandpa and a bunch of other people who were suddenly just out there on the field. The ref blew the whistle and we were supposed to start playing again, but most of our team had their eyes glued on the stretcher. Their number ten got a yellow card and was now sitting on the sidelines crying. The ref placed the ball down and we got a free kick which Amber took and scored on but nobody cared, even Otto who always goes crazy when we get a goal.

Shawna Sully went in as goalie for the rest of the game and she did a good job even though they did end up scoring two goals. We won five to two but no one was celebrating. Madeline's mom called Courtney's dad on the cellphone and we found out that Madeline had torn a bunch of ligaments and was going to have her leg in a cast for two months and be on crutches. Nammy had come to the game but she got there late and missed the whole thing. We all told her what happened and she just couldn't believe it. Most of her questions were about Madeline's health insurance and who would pay for all the costs. Mr. Bilsesser kept saying it wouldn't be a problem but it was obvious Nammy didn't believe him because she wouldn't get off it.

It wasn't until we were home and I'd put my uniform in the washing machine, which I always did even though it never got dirty, that I realized I was now the back-up goalie. Before I'd been the back-up to the back-up, which was very safe. Now it was possible I might have to actually play. Madeline usually came out near the end of the second half if we were winning and Shawna got to have some time on the field. A few times Madeline had even changed shirts and gone out to be a forward or a mid-fielder.

Just thinking about my new responsibilities made me feel sick. I took my temperature three times and even though I felt all hot and sweaty I didn't have a fever which was hard to believe.

I lay in bed for hours staring at the ceiling. I only fell asleep that night after I'd made the decision to talk to Otto the next day about changing positions. If he wouldn't, I made a plan to climb up onto our roof and jump off into the front yard. I'd break my legs for sure and everything would be okay.

TWENTY-SIX

Otto wouldn't even discuss me changing positions. And when I came home from school and looked up at our roof I realized it just wasn't high enough to do any damage. Plus I'm afraid of ladders so I don't know how I'd even get up there to begin with.

By lunchtime the next day Madeline was back in class and the whole team sat together with her in the cafeteria. We all told the story of how she got hurt but I ended up with the official version because I could remember the little things like the fact that Number Ten had earrings with ladybugs on them, and girls like Mona Baron got too excited and just went right to the injury part.

Madeline was really sad about missing the rest of the season because she was one of the players who really loved the sport and looked forward to it all year long. But her life wasn't all rotten now. Her dad went out and got her a whole new video game system which she'd really wanted and her big sister had to switch rooms with her because Madeline's bedroom was upstairs in what was really supposed to be an attic or something. The big sister's room had it's own bathroom and was right next to the kitchen and Madeline said she hoped she never had to trade back and her sister would just go off to college and she'd have it for real. Helen Herlihy told her to limp for a long time after the cast came off and complain about the stairs and it might work.

I didn't change into my practice clothes right after the last class like I'm supposed to, but instead I went straight out to the field so I could discuss my new plan with Otto. He cut me off right away and told me to go get dressed. He said I was a goalie and we were now halfway through the season and there was no turning back. I thought about just sneaking off and heading home but when I saw everyone come out of the gym I couldn't. Madeline was on her crutches with the rest of the team because she wanted to watch us practice and she smiled big when she saw me and said she was giving me her goalie shirt. The last thing I wanted to do was wear it and not just because at this point it obviously wasn't lucky. I acted like I was happy and Courtney made me put the thing on. Of course it was way too big and on my body looked like a dress.

But the worst part was yet to come. We ran around for awhile and then did some kicking drills like regular and then Otto had us scrimmage. Only now the two goalies weren't Madeline and Shawna. They were me and Shawna. Once I realized I was going to be in the line of fire I went straight to Courtney. I didn't even have to say anything because she could see I was even more pale than usual and my hands were trembling like Nammy's do when she tries to thread a needle or put on one of her dangling earrings.

Courtney whispered that she'd make sure she was on my side and no ball would get anywhere near my goal. I could tell she meant it and since she was the best player on the team I stopped breathing so funny. As I walked down to my end of the field I tried to figure out how I'd ended up in this mess. I had all these people now counting on me to do something that was just plain against my every natural instinct. What sane person wants to throw their body in the path of a fast moving leather ball? It was just ridiculous.

Otto blew his whistle and Courtney was true to her word. She scrambled around the field as if her life depended on making sure no one got a shot at my net. At first I just stared out at the game in rigid fear. But whenever the ball looked like it might be coming anywhere near me some strange reflex went off and I started yelling like crazy to my teammates to go get it first. I shouted so much that at the end of the twenty minutes, which felt like twenty hours, I had almost completely lost my voice. Only when Otto started to laugh did I realize how crazy I must have sounded.

But losing my voice wasn't my only problem. It turned out that they'd never taken a shot on goal while I was in it. Mostly this was because Courtney played as if she were in the Olympics, but according to our coach that wasn't the only reason. Otto gave a speech about the importance of communication on the field, and how great it was that I was back there hollering my head off. I saw Madeline who was sitting on the bench with her cast stare down at the ground for just a second. She was always really quiet when she played and now she must have felt sad about it. Then I realized Shawna Sully was chewing on her thumbnail and looking worried. That's when I realized I was in real trouble.

Instead of showing them all what a loser I was, I'd supposedly taught them something. I couldn't believe it. On top of everything else, Courtney looked as happy as I'd seen her. Otto took her aside and told her what a great job she'd done and her face turned all red and she just smiled and smiled. We ended practice with a few fast laps around the field, which didn't feel like anything anymore.

As I walked back to the gym I thought about how I'd been tricked into this whole thing. I never wanted to kick a soccer ball and now I could boot one almost half-way across the field. I've never liked to run and now I could do a dozen laps without even breathing different. I was eating more, sleeping less, and I had more energy. And there was nothing I could do about it.

I'd completely lost control of my own life.

TWENTY-SEVEN

A week later we had our next game. I was up almost the whole night before worrying about everything from hunger in Central Africa to whether termites were eating the foundation of Nammy's house and causing certain and irreparable damage to what was already not a stable structure. I wouldn't allow myself to even think about soccer because I knew I'd be breathing into a paper bag covered with cold sweat if I did.

As it turned out I didn't have anything to worry about. Shawna Sully played the whole game as our goalie and we won three to nothing. Nammy showed up just before half-time with her lawn chair and a big "Go Eagles" sign. She'd cut her black wig shorter again and she was starting to look more normal. Either that or I was just getting used to her with straight synthetic hair.

Courtney had a great game and scored two of the three goals and it wasn't even because she was protecting me. Shawna yelled at our team throughout the game to get in position and Otto was very happy when it was all over. He took us back behind the gym and made us sit in a circle and he went around and told each of us what we'd contributed to the victory. I was thinking my big contribution, as always, was the fact that I didn't play, but he had other ideas. He said that my courage in the face of Madeline's injury had been an inspiration to the team. And then on behalf of the team he thanked me.

No one on the planet has ever called me courageous. I was almost held back in kindergarten because all year I refused to go up the stairs to the library. Every Thursday they took our class up there, and since I refused to go I had to wait in the nurse's office. I failed beginning swimming class three different summers because I wouldn't move out of the shallow end. Plus I've called 911 from our house enough times that I know two of the operators by their first names. I've been so afraid of so many different things I'm afraid to even think about it because I know I'll freak out.

But Otto wasn't kidding. He meant it about my being courageous. And I don't think it was because he was a foreigner and didn't always understand what I said or did. He really thought I somehow had helped my teammates. Go figure.

Having someone call you something can make you feel more that way. I guess that's why it's important to not call a chubby kid 'Fatso.' Or a kid with bad muscle control 'Spaz.' You just keep them in that condition. But the opposite is true, too. If you tell someone they are something good, they can be more of it. After Otto called me brave I started to feel like I wasn't the biggest chicken on the planet. It was kind of like the

Cowardly Lion in "The Wizard of Oz." He gave me my courage.

Which isn't to say I was now patrolling the neighborhood at night looking for bad guys or killing the spiders in the bathroom. But I do think I didn't feel like I was going to jump out of my own skin as much as usual.

And then I used the same approach with Nammy. She'd bought some orange dye at the market in a little box and decided to change the color of the curtains in the living room just to brighten up the place. They were once white and now were oatmeal, which is just another way of saying they were really faded and kind of old and dirty. She loaded them up into the washing machine, which was where she decided to dye them.

I think if you do it that way, you're supposed to take them out right away and maybe use the gentle cycle or something. But Nammy was watching some program on TV where people cook food while they are dressed up as farm animals and she had the machine set on the regular wash. When she unloaded the curtains they'd been in for a few hours and kind of hardened onto the sidewalls of the drum. She yelled for me to help and I came to the back porch and you could see right away that it didn't work right. Neither of us said anything but after we got the curtains out of the dryer it was pretty obvious the orange dye had stuck only in spots and that the fabric wasn't strong enough to take the violence of a washing machine. They now looked like something you'd see on the back window of a hippie van that had been driving around for a million years and parking in the sun. On top of the color problem, tons of the thread had come out and hung loose like a million cats had clawed them.

Nammy stared at the curtains and before she could say anything I shrieked about how great they now were. I picked up one of the panels and held it close and said they looked so cool with all the different shades of orange in different places and the loose strings dangling. I said no one would ever be able to duplicate the look. It was so original. So modern. Nammy looked at me and then at the curtains and then back at me. I was smiling big and running my hand over the wrecked material.

Suddenly Nammy started smiling, too. She looked right at me, "You really like them?"

I nodded.

"Oh yeah. They look tie-dyed!"

Nammy nodded now, too.

"Yeah. That's kind of what I was going after."

We put them up together which was harder than taking them down. I even climbed up onto a ladder which I hate to do. When I finally got off Nammy was admiring the new look, pleased as could be. She gushed, "They're original, that's for sure!"

I was so glad to see that she was happy I didn't even care that our living room now looked like a tiger lived in the house.

I slipped my hand into hers and I meant it when I said, "Who'd want it any other way?"

TWENTY-EIGHT

We practiced all the next week in the rain and by the time we had our game on Friday half the team had colds and were coughing up really gross-colored stuff. Anyone who looked at our team would have picked me as the first one to get sick, but even though everyone around me was all snotty, I felt totally normal. Courtney went through the whole third grade without missing a day of school and got a special prize and everything and now even she didn't feel well.

There were only three games left in the season and Otto told us all kinds of stories of people he knew in Hungary who played when they were half out of their minds with fevers and broken legs and all kinds of other health problems. I think he thought he was being inspiring but he only made me think that they were crazy over in Hungary. He knew people who got up out of hospital beds and went out onto the soccer field. We have all these rules at school and one of them is that if you haven't been to class during the day you aren't allowed to be in an after-school sport.

Unbelievably, on game day everyone on our team was there in the morning, even Rosie Chung who had taken so much cold medicine she fell asleep in second period. The nurse sent her home so we knew right away we didn't have our regular left fullback. After lunch three other girls were in the office calling their parents. Amber Rizzo had a sore throat and Helen Herlihy had thrown up in history. Chelsea Luzzato coughed so much the science teacher made her leave. I felt bad for them but all I really cared about was Shawna Sully. She had an awful cold but there didn't seem to be anything else wrong with her. I brought her orange juice from the snack bar at our morning break and then stood in line to get her lunch so she'd have as much time as possible off her feet. If nothing else I was hoping I'd catch whatever she had and then there would be no question of ever putting me in the game.

But I continued to feel fine and she felt worse as the day wore on. We took a bus across town to Bailey Middle School and Shawna blew her nose about a million times on the way over. Fortunately Otto wasn't feeling very well by this point so he didn't seem to notice. We'd beaten Bailey the first time around four weeks ago. They had a few good players and then a bunch of girls who just didn't look like they cared about the game. Maybe it was because their coach didn't seem very interested. They had a man like us but he didn't look anything like Otto. In fairness to their coach, no one did. But he didn't act like Otto either. He paced on the sidelines and barely spoke, with a sour face that said he was defeated before he'd even gotten started.

Otto had us go really easy during our warm-ups because half the team went into coughing fits once they started breathing hard. I faked a few sneezes but no one paid any attention. The first half of the game went by without a problem and we scored twice and they only did once so everything was okay. Shawna didn't look so great but neither did anyone else, really. Courtney wasn't beating anyone to the ball like she usually did and she twice told Otto she was sorry and he just nodded and told her to do her best.

We had about eight minutes left to go in the game when Shawna's face suddenly turned all red. She started coughing hard and she looked like a fish that had flopped out of its tank. Her mouth was open and she was gasping for air. I noticed right away because I had my eyes on her the whole time. At first I just hoped she'd settle down, but then I realized something was really wrong. I ran over to Otto and pointed out her problem. Right when I did this Shawna fell to her knees. Since the ball wasn't anywhere near her this wasn't a good sign. Courtney, who has that weird talent where she sees the field at all times, somehow saw what was going on behind her and purposely kicked the ball out of bounds so that Otto could get the ref's attention. He stopped the clock and let Otto go out onto the field. At this point Shawna was all curled up like a pill bug and I couldn't even see her red face anymore.

That's when I found out that Shawna had asthma. Her mother showed up out of nowhere and was on the field and then running to her car for an inhaler. Half our team just sunk to the grass because the truth was they were now all having trouble breathing. The next part happened so fast I wasn't sure what was going on. Shawna came off the field sort of propped up by Otto and the ref. She leaned way more on Otto than the old ref and I was hoping she felt well enough to remember what his strong Hungarian shoulder felt like. Once she was on the bench, they got her goalie shirt off and before I knew what was happening Otto pulled it over my head and someone pushed me out onto the field.

I ran to the goalie box because the ref was already blowing the whistle to get the game going again. Now up until this point it didn't seem that the Bailey Middle School girls even cared about the sport. But once they put me in they must have sensed they had a chance. Out of nowhere they came alive and gained control of the ball. I watched helplessly as they charged as a team straight down towards me. I started yelling as if my life depended on it. Courtney came alive and went after the ball but the rest of the team was too tired and too sick to really follow instructions. It looked to me like they were all moving in slow motion.

But the ball wasn't. Their fastest forward went right past our sweeper and crossed to the middle. Courtney sprinted but she couldn't get there soon enough. I watched in horror as their strongest player took a shot. Once the ball connected with her foot I instinctively dove out of the way.

As luck would have it, her kick had some topspin. Instead of going straight into the net, it curved over two feet and hit the back of my extended legs. By trying to get out of the way I'd made a save. Once the ball hit me I fell on top of it like a kid wrestling a piñata to the grass to hoard all the candy.

When I got up I saw Otto on the sidelines cheering. Even though Shawna had her inhaler in her mouth she was pumping her fist.

The last thing I wanted to do was put the ball back in play but it was obvious I had to. Fortunately I can actually kick the thing. I cleared it out to the center of the field and I could tell by the look on Courtney's face she'd keep it away from me for the rest of the game no matter what. She got a yellow card a few minutes later for tripping a girl who had the ball and I could see she wasn't even sorry. When the ref blew the whistle three times to let us know the game was over I still couldn't believe I was actually on the field playing. I stayed in front of the box looking out in horror as if the other team was still coming at me. It wasn't until Courtney and Drina came running over to get me that I really believed it was over.

As we headed to the sidelines it started to rain which turned out to be a good thing because I was sort of crying and that way you couldn't tell the raindrops from my tears. Shawna and Otto hugged me the hardest and it wasn't until we were back in the bus driving home that I realized what had happened.

I'd played in a soccer game.

TWENTY-NINE

Shawna was feeling okay for our next game and she played the whole time and we won without a problem. That left only one game in the season and it was against Franklin Middle School and the dreaded Ashley Aiken. Since the only time we'd lost was to Franklin, we had a lot to prove. Especially because they had the same record as us meaning they were also eight and one. They had lost to Bailey Middle School and we'd beaten them. If we could win our last game against Franklin we'd be nine and one and they'd be eight and two, and for the first time in twenty years we'd have the best record in the league.

Of course Otto thought we could do it. Most of the girls didn't have drippy red noses anymore and only a handful of them were still coughing. Since Shawna's asthma attack she had a new inhaler and she didn't run laps with us at the beginning of practice, because no one wanted her to push too hard.

It had been awhile since Madeline had hurt her leg and I was okay now being the goalie in our scrimmages. Most of the time if someone kicked right at me I ducked or jumped out of the way, which is exactly what I was not supposed to do. But every now and then I actually blocked a shot and I could kick the ball out as far as Shawna could so it wasn't like I was a total loser. Plus because I always was yelling my head off out on the field everyone on our team started yelling at each other which turned out to be a good thing. At least Otto said it was.

This time the game was at our school. Nammy got up that morning and when I came out of my room she'd made me pancakes with chocolate chips inside. I couldn't remember her ever making pancakes my whole life and if she did it was never at seven in the morning. She'd also put green food coloring in the batter so they didn't really look that good but I didn't even have to pretend they tasted great because they really did. After I ate she went back to bed because she wasn't a morning person but she blew me a kiss and said she was proud of me.

At school everyone knew this was our big game day. The cool boys even came over and talked to us before our first class. They always came over and tried to talk to Courtney but now they were talking to all of us. Stephen Boyd leaned against my locker and asked me a few soccer questions and I got all nervous not because they were goalie questions, but because he always made me feel that way. Stephen was the smartest boy in our grade but he somehow was cool which wasn't normally the way it worked. He wasn't very tall but had big brown eyes that made it impossible for me to look at him because I got this weird feeling in my stomach when I did. So I didn't look at him or answer any of his questions and he finally got the message and headed off to math class. After he was gone I got really mad at myself because he probably now knew I liked him since I wouldn't talk to him.

Our whole team sat together at lunch and we tried not to think about the game. We mostly concentrated on Otto. He was supposed to go back home to Europe in two months and all of us felt sick about it. Courtney had been reading up on Hungary and it was amazing how much she knew about the place. We were all shocked. She memorized a few sayings and taught us all to say "Nagyon szepen koszonom, kocsi," which in Hungarian means, "Thank you so much, coach." We were probably all saying it wrong but after awhile it became a chant and we were yelling the crazy sounding words so loud that Mr. Edelman came over and told us to keep it down because we were giving him a big headache. Mr. Edelman teaches music and the kids give him big headaches every day during class because they play so poorly. This makes him extra sensitive to noise during lunch hour.

When we went to the gym to change into our uniforms at the end of the day we did some more Hungarian chanting but we got quiet when we went outside and saw Otto because we wanted it to be a surprise. There were more people at this game than at any of our other games put together. Courtney's dad was there like always, but this time her mom came, too. And halfway through the game her brothers Ned and Wally walked over from the high school to watch. Jose was standing on the sidelines when we ran out and he waved to me and called out my name. I hadn't seen him since he left school and got the job in the ambulance so I was really happy to see he was wearing a white uniform and that he looked really good.

Clyde was there, too. I hadn't been to visit him as much as I did before soccer but I still stopped by on the weekends and sometimes I took out his recycling and put in a load of his laundry. I was really honored that he showed up because he hates crowds and I think he hates sports, too. Plus I knew he'd taken his life into his own hands by driving to the field because I saw his big old car parked all crooked in the distance with one wheel up on the curb.

Our science teacher, Ms. Biculos, came across the parking lot to watch in her high heels and one of her totally impractical tight skirts. The principal, Mr. Hockstatter, showed up a few minutes later and he went and sat with her in the bleachers. Coach Moshofsky brought out a big cooler of water, which was nice, because normally we bring all of our own stuff. She smiled at me and said good luck and I could tell she really meant it because we'd gotten to be friends after the deal we made during basketball season. Jessica Pendergast was there with a bunch of girls from the drill team. She was the girl I'd tripped during basketball try-outs and she was just now done with physical therapy and really happy to not be wearing her brace anymore. She gave us all a wave and shouted "Go Eagles." Behind Jessica, the cool boys all came together in a herd like a group of livestock. I saw Stephen Boyd in the center of the pack and I tried to remember what he'd asked me in the morning but that already seemed like ten years ago. They sat up on the top of the bleachers all in a row and I looked up and thought that they looked like birds on an electrical wire.

Even my and Courtney's advisor, Mrs. Wiener, stayed after school for the game. She always got everything wrong, so she showed up late and was all flustered and waving her thin arms around like she does when she gets nervous. Madeline was there in her cast and so was her whole family which was really nice of them since I know they were all really disappointed that she wasn't going to be out on the field.

The only one who wasn't there was Nammy which surprised me. At first I kept looking out at the street thinking she was going to show up, but after awhile I just quit. I had too many other things to worry about.

THIRTY

Ashley Aiken was the first one off the new bus from Franklin. It didn't seem possible but she'd grown since I last saw her. She had always been big for her age but now she looked like a giant or something. Everyone I'd ever seen play soccer in our league wore black shoes that everyone knows you buy down at Comb's Shoe Store. Everyone that is except Ashley. She now had on red leather shoes with black stripes that forced you to just stare at her huge feet. I guess her parents had sent away for them from a catalog and they were specially made probably because her feet were so enormous. So right away all of us were talking about the red shoes which wasn't good for our concentration but if you get that many teenage girls together and it's the first time they've seen a new shoe I don't see how anything else could happen.

During warm-ups it was my job to go after the balls that were kicked wide of the goal. I also kicked out to the team so Ashley couldn't help but see that now I could boot the ball pretty far. But that didn't stop her from giving me one of her sneers. Usually I looked away but this time I didn't. I could tell it bothered her.

Otto called us over to the sidelines early and he gave us a longer talk than normal, where he said to concentrate and play as a team and pass and communicate and a bunch of other stuff that you hear but don't hear because it's not like you haven't been told the same things a thousand times. But we all acted interested because it was Otto and just watching his mouth move was pretty entertaining.

Courtney and Helen Herlihy were our captains and they went out to the middle of the field and had to shake hands with Ashley and another girl who looked sort of nice. Courtney said afterwards that Ashley "trash-talked" when the ref couldn't hear but I don't know what she said.

No one scored in the first twenty minutes of the game and the teams seemed to be evenly matched. Courtney led a few good drives down to their goal and we took a bunch of shots that could have gone in if the wind had been right or luck had been in our favor. They had a couple of chances to score on us but Shawna was all over the ball and once even blocked a shot that was kicked so hard it knocked her off her feet. I was worried right away that she was hurt but she got up and shook it off and was okay.

At halftime there was still no score and Otto told us when we were off sitting in our circle, that he thought the only way to make a goal in this type of game was with "a breakaway." Both teams were playing it smart and he said we had to wait until they had all pushed up and their defenders were way forward and then send someone blowing right by them. We all knew that "someone" was Courtney and she listened and nodded her head and everyone got the picture to pass to her and let her use her speed.

Unfortunately, I think the coach on the other side was saying the same thing because they came out after halftime and scored within the first five minutes on a breakaway led by Ashley and her big red feet. Shawna tried to block the shot but it was just impossible because the kick was perfectly placed in the top left corner right over her head. Falling behind made our team play harder and only a few minutes later Courtney scored on a header and we were back to a tie game.

Once the scoring starts sometimes it just breaks some kind of voodoo that's on the field because right away we scored again. We all went crazy jumping up and down because now we were ahead two to one. This time it was Maria Morales who scored, which was great because she was a quiet player all year and just one of those solid athletes who does everything right but never shows off about it.

When Maria scored we all started hugging on the sidelines even though there was lots of time left and we really shouldn't have been celebrating like that. After that Franklin substituted three players and we must have let down our guard because they then scored twice in a row. We went from being up by one to being down by one in a matter of minutes. All of a sudden Shawna didn't look good and I think the pressure was getting to her or something.

It was three-to-two with five minutes left in the game and our players knew what they had to do. Courtney got the ball away and scored and we were back to a tie game. It was now three all. At this point all of our stomachs were in knots. We had to score. I guess the pressure was too much for Shawna. I could see her put her hands on her knees and hang her head and I knew right away she was breathing funny. I turned to the bleachers behind me and saw her mom and stepdad and they could tell something was wrong. Shawna's mom started fishing around in her purse for the inhaler and I had to tell Otto.

Shawna came off the field right away and I started to put on her goalie shirt. I saw Otto look at the bench where Martha Metzler was sitting with Jasmine Assad and Heather Clerkin and I knew what he was thinking. All of them were good athletes and none of them were afraid of the ball. He looked back at me and I stopped putting on the goalie jersey. He was right. Too much was at stake.

But instead he just grinned and yelled for me to get out on the field.

THIRTY-ONE

Once I was on the grass Courtney came running over and said she promised she'd keep them all away. I just nodded because my throat was too constricted to even speak. I looked out at Ashley and caught her eye and she smiled. It was a scary smile. The kind of smile that said she now believed fortune had turned her way. On the sidelines Shawna had the inhaler in her mouth and her head between her knees and didn't look like she'd be coming to my rescue.

The ref put the ball back in play and I could feel our whole team tense up, especially our defensive players. Because I was now on the field everyone on my team looked like our school was on fire. If there's one thing I know it's fear. And I could really see it in their faces. All the spectators must have felt it too because everyone on our side got to their feet, even Clyde who had a cane and was pretty wobbly. Courtney's dad was shouting out all kinds of encouraging stuff and I couldn't even look over there anymore because I was afraid I'd throw up or something. Otto yelled to the ref for time remaining and he yelled back, four minutes.

I did the math. I only had 240 seconds. It seemed like eternity.

It was. But of course, right away, Courtney, who was already playing her heart out, took her game to a higher level. After about two minutes she stole the ball away from one of their best players and even though as a team we're supposed to pass, pass, pass, she just went straight down the field and scored. We all went crazy. Everyone was jumping around on top of everyone else and the fans were cheering and I started to get the feeling back in my arms and legs. We were now ahead by one goal, four to three, but there was still about a minute left in the game. All we had to do was keep the ball away from our goal.

That turned out to be impossible. Ashley, looking like a big truck with red wheels, got the soccer ball and came charging down the field right at me. I started yelling to everyone to get in there and kick it away but she moved right by our players as if she'd mow down anyone who stood in her way. Just when I thought Rosie was going to get the ball away, Ashley passed off to another player and now the two of them were driving to the goal. Courtney was over on the far side of the field and she sprinted for Ashley. The other player passed it back to Ashley and now Courtney and Ashley and the ball were all heading right for me. I had my eyes glued to their feet, watching and waiting for the kick. But it didn't come. Instead, just as both girls crossed over the line into the penalty box, Ashley purposely turned inward and ran into Courtney's legs making it look as if she had been tripped. She then flew up into the air and landed in a heap on the grass.

Of course the ref blew his whistle. And of course Ashley had drawn the foul. Courtney started yelling that it wasn't her fault, which of course it wasn't, and Otto got so red in the face yelling about the bad call I thought he was going to burst. When a foul occurs in the box it means only one thing, a penalty kick. And that meant it was going to be just me and Ashley, one on one, battling it out for the game.

I looked over at the bench and Shawna's asthma appeared to momentarily get even worse. Everyone was on their feet and I swear it looked like some of the adults were praying. Up in the bleachers Clyde raised his cane and Jose, who was only a row away, was shouting something but I couldn't hear. Ashley got up from the ground and limped around a little bit as if she'd been injured for life. Before she took her place on the penalty kick spot she looked over at me and grinned. I wanted to cry because I knew she fell on purpose and I knew she wanted to make me look like a fool and because I was afraid of the ball and her kick and the crowd. I was also afraid of Clowns. Big trees. Any room that's dark. Thunder. Firecrackers. Cats. Motorcycles. Bees. Snowballs. Most knives. Some forks. Car wash places. Elevators. Hamsters. The guys behind the sushi counter who yell when you come in. Certain shades of purple. Alleys. Sprinkler heads. Any dog bigger than a cat and I already explained about the cats. Men in beards. Men in moustaches. Blood. Catsup (because it looks like blood). And most kinds of cheese.

And now all of it was in the ball that the ref placed on

the ground. All of it was right in front of me.

But when I looked out, the one thing I wasn't afraid of suddenly was Ashley. She had her cool red shoes and her expensive haircut and her braces had come off before anyone else so she had teeth like in the movies but I didn't see a whole bunch of people chanting her name or waving their canes. I didn't see hugging and trembling and freaking out because she got to take a shot on me. She wasn't wearing shoes some nice family had bought for her and she probably didn't have a lucky rock in her right sock.

So I looked her right in the eye. Now I'd noticed something in all those hours I'd spent bringing back the balls for Shawna. When players take a shot on goal, they usually look, for just the smallest of moments, at the spot they are aiming for. If they were going to kick right corner, they'd look there, just to put it in their brain. Now they may then look down at the ground, look up at the goalie, look off into space, but they'd revealed their plan. I watched every twitch of her eyes and for just a flash, just a glance, she looked left.

Ashley pulled her hair back and charged at the ball. As her foot made contact I didn't wait. I forgot about how hard the dirt was and how much a ball hurt when it hit you. I forgot about all of the things that make me afraid and I dove left.

THIRTY-TWO

Which doesn't make me a great goalie or anything, but I blocked her shot. And I have to say, when that ball hit my hands, it really, really, really hurt. But I didn't feel it for long because two seconds later the ref blew the whistle three times and the game was over and everyone was jumping on top of me (which didn't feel that great either), but I was too excited to tell them to get off. Otto ran out onto the field and so did all our players and Shawna's asthma started calming down and the next thing I knew Courtney's parents were hugging me and Clyde was out there and Jose and all the cool boys and it looked like the pictures I've seen of New Year's Eve in big cities where everyone is going nuts.

So we went crazy for a while and then when we sort of calmed down Otto took us players over to the side of the field alone and said that he was so proud of us and Courtney gave us all a look and we said together, "Nagyon szepen koszonom, kocsi," which we think in Hungarian means, "Thank you so much, coach." At first we kind of regretted it because he got tears in his eyes and couldn't speak which made us all feel really weird. But then he looked away and coughed and acted like he had a medical problem and everything was okay.

After we said good-bye to everyone about a million times we got in Courtney's parents' car which was a squeeze because we had Ned and Wally, too. I tried to call Nammy on their cell phone to tell her the good news but she didn't answer, which was just like her because she says the only people who call after dark want to sell her a newspaper subscription or get her to change her long distance telephone service. I told Mr. and Mrs. Bilsesser that I didn't ever remember being as happy and they all laughed and Courtney said she'd never been as happy, too, which I found hard to believe because she's won all kinds of things but I didn't bring that up. I was so excited by the time I got home I was singing when I ran to the front door. I keep my house key on a chain on my backpack and I opened the door and burst inside calling out for Nammy.

It took me a few seconds to realize it was dark inside which was weird and the TV wasn't on. I flipped on the lights by the door and I saw right away that the stuff was still out from the chocolate chip pancakes Nammy made in the morning. That wasn't so strange though because sometimes she's not very good about cleaning up. I yelled for her again and didn't get an answer so I went right to her room. I turned on the lights and there she was lying in bed. I started to shout right away that we'd won but the words got stuck in my mouth because I could tell everything was all wrong. I fell to my knees against the bed and my body went numb and it was as if I was there but I wasn't there all at the same time. I buried my head in the pillows by her hair and the smell of the white face cream she always wore was strong and my hand touched her bare shoulder and it was cold and I knew she had left me.

I realize now that I'd been afraid that this would happen my whole life even though I'd never even once thought about it. I just knew that one day she wouldn't be shuffling around the house singing her songs about working on a railroad or flying a kite. And even though my legs were all dirty from the field I climbed up onto the bed to be right next to her and to tell her that I loved her and that I didn't want her to go and that I was going to miss her forever and ever and then some more. I said it wasn't fair for her to leave me and if she did she should have taken me with her. I said she'd been a good Nammy. She'd been a great Nammy. She'd been everything to me.

I don't know how long I stayed like that because I don't remember much else about the night. I know I called Courtney and her parents came over and her mother is a doctor so she knew what to do and they took me home and I stayed there for a whole week but I didn't go to school or anything.

My Uncle Arnold flew out from back east and there were all kinds of meetings with people but I never went to them and then finally they sat me down at Izzy's Deli in the red booth in the back and told me that Nammy had a heart attack and died right away, which of course I already knew, but I think they thought it would make me feel better to hear them say it all together with warm waffles on the table. They said she would have been eighty-six years old on her birthday, which I didn't know. She was always saying she was younger. I realized then that she slept a lot because she was kind of old, not just because she was getting over the flu like she always said.

While we were in the restaurant they gave me a bunch of choices about my life which was good because they wanted me to be part of what was going to happen. All kinds of people had said they would take care of me, even Clyde which was really nice. Uncle Arnold was prepared to take me back east and he didn't offer just because by law he had to or something. Even the Bilsesser's said I could come live at their house and they'd convert their garage and move the boys outside so there would be more room. But I decided I didn't want any of it.

I'd read about a boarding school that was only a few hours away. Kids came from all around the country to go there and it looked very safe and orderly and what I liked most was that if I went there everyone would be on their own just like me. The kids in the pictures didn't look mean and none of them knew me or Nammy or anything about my life, which made me feel better about things. I was afraid to tell Courtney but when I did she didn't get mad. She sat for a long time in silence and then she said that she wanted to go, too. Otto was going back to Hungary and she couldn't take the idea of both of us being gone. Since she couldn't immigrate to Europe, she'd work on her parents for boarding school

I was surprised everybody said yes to our plan. It was decided that I'd come back and stay with Courtney's family on holidays and I'd see Clyde and Jose and all my friends. We'd sell Nammy's house so there would be money for me all the way through college and a lawyer was going to be in charge of it because one of Nammy's ex-husbands had shown up and was sniffing around to see if he'd get anything. There was still a term left of the school year and the boarding school said they had room so I was going to go up right away and begin. Courtney would start the next fall.

Everyone was really nice to me when they found out I was leaving. The soccer girls had a party at Pietro's Pizza Place and Madeline gave me her goalie shirt to keep for good. Otto came and he sat with us, not the parents, which was so great. He was leaving in a week for Hungary so it was a good-bye party for both of us. Everyone cried at the end and I think it was mostly about saying good-bye to Otto but I didn't hold that against any of them.

My advisor at school, Mrs. Wiener, got all weepy and said she'd like to give me something to remember Eleanor Roosevelt Middle School by and I said I'd really love to have a book in the library called "Anomalies of Nature." I told her no one had checked out the book for twenty-nine years so I didn't think anyone would miss it. When she asked why I wanted the book I told her I thought I was an anomaly of nature. After that they didn't have a problem with me taking it.

Right before I left, Ms. Biculos named me as a finalist in the science fair, which meant that my project on bread mold went on to the county competition. I think she felt sorry for me or something because my experiment sucked and everyone knew it. Coach Moshofsky wrote one of my recommendations for boarding school and so did Otto and my English teacher, Mrs. Holsing, who thought I was way smarter than I was just because I actually read the books and thought about them for a few minutes. Even Ashley Aiken and her parents dropped off a box of fancy chocolates for me, which just proves that people were gray and not all jerks all the time.

I had to be careful about what to take to the new school because there was only so much I could bring. I knew I wanted the trunk with my Mom's stuff for sure, and then a second trunk of things from Nammy which included her black wig and her TV changer. But when I went through my own stuff I realized that my soccer shoes and the little medal I got for being on the team meant the most to me. I decided I was going to try and play at the new school. I was glad I could run two miles without really getting tired and that I could kick a ball thirty yards.

When I was packing I made a promise to myself. When I got scared I was going to act like I was in the goalie box and I was going to look for signs of what would happen. Maybe I'd see them. Maybe I wouldn't. But I wasn't going to quit.

My new secret was going to be that I'd seen more than most kids my age. And despite that, I wasn't always going to be afraid.

THIRTY-THREE

In the years that passed I came to love the sport of soccer. By the time I graduated from high school, I was captain of the team (with Courtney) and voted All-League and then All-State in a coaches' poll. I went on to play soccer in college on a full scholarship, which is where I am today.

Courtney lettered in three sports in high school and now studies Slavic History at an excellent university back east. We still speak on the phone once a week and her parents and brothers are my family now, along with a big group of friends who have been there for me for the last eight years. Clyde is in his nineties and still as feisty as ever. The state took away his driver's license a few years ago so the local streets are safe today. Jose now works at the hospital in the x-ray division. His oldest son is pre-med at the local college. Mr. Hockstatter ended up getting divorced and then a few years later, married Ms. Biculos, who now is called Ms. Biculos-Hockstatter, which is really a mouthful.

Although I have always had many interests and hobbies, soccer has been the most steady and stable thing in my life since the eighth grade. I cannot imagine where I would be today without the game. I have now traveled around most of the country playing in matches, and I know many of my closest friends because of the sport.

But I will never forget the time when I couldn't kick a ball. Or run for more than a block. I will never forget the person who was afraid of the world. Most of all, I will never forget the team and the people who were there to help that girl. Along with my beloved Nammy, they are always there with me every step of the way. They give me strength when I can't see what's in the shadows. And they make it possible for me to live my life in the light.

TEST YOURSELF...ARE YOU A PROFESSIONAL READER?

Chapters 1-3

After reading Chapter 1, what can you interpret about Sasha's friendship with Courtney? Her relationship with Nammy?

Sasha is an expert on scary things. What scares her more than anything else?

Why does Nammy own three automatic cat box cleaners and not even one cat?

ESSAY

Describe the 'ice age' in this book. Have you ever had a similar experience with one of your friends? What did you learn from your 'ice age'?

Chapters 4-6

From what you know about Courtney's personality, would you think she would be successful in the science fair? Use examples form the text to back your choice.

How did Courtney attempt to turn Sasha on to soccer?

Why doesn't Nammy have ice cream in the house anymore?

ESSAY

Did Sasha achieve what she originally planned by trying out for the basketball team? What did she receive? Was Courtney satisfied that Sasha tried out?

Chapters 7-9

What reasons did Sasha give for being afraid of Courtney's older brother, Ned?

Who was the person who figured out Courtney's plan to train Sasha? How did he/she figure this out?

Who is Ashley Aiken?

ESSAY

Why didn't Sasha want Ashley Aiken to see her shopping at the Salvation Army? Do you think it was right for Ashley to laugh at Sasha when she saw her at the Salvation Army? Explain the reasoning behind your answer.

Chapters 10-12

Why did Nammy decide to donate 'stuff' to the Salvation Army?

Who did Sasha blame for Nammy being brought to the police station? Why did she blame this person?

What does Sasha do when she wants to feel like 'everything is okay in the world'?

ESSAY

Otto's presence brings out the best of Courtney's soccer skills. Name someone in your life that encourages you to excel. Explain why this person is so important to you. Why do you want to do well for this person?

Chapters 13-15

What was the 'only thing that Sasha was good at'?

Why did Sasha claim that she never wanted to eat another bacon cheeseburger again?

What was the only sport that Nammy understood? Why?

ESSAY

Sasha broke down the players at tryouts into four groups. Name them. Which group did Sasha place herself into? According to Sasha, who was the most annoying type of player that tried out?

Chapters 16-18

Sasha had a funny way of showing that she was excited to make the soccer team. How did she show her emotions?

Would Otto have been impressed by Sasha's eating habits? What did her daily breakfast consist of?

Why was Sasha excited when Otto told her that she would be the third string goalie?

ESSAY

What fears caused Sasha to formulate a plan to change the game of soccer? What did Sasha have in mind on her 'crusade' to change the sport? What did these plans reveal about Sasha's personality?

Chapters 19-21

In Sasha's cafeteria lunch, what did 'MM' stand for? Was Sasha a big fan of the 'MM'?

What was the cause of Nammy's sudden stomach-ache?

Who was Hilly Saunders? Why did Otto remind Sasha of her?

ESSAY

Sasha says that this is the first time since 'Campfire Girls' that she has been a part of a group. She also claims that 'doing things in a group can make you do way more than you'd do on your own'? Why do you think this is true? Can you think of an example in your life when you did more because you were in a group?

Chapters 22-24

How did Nammy show Sasha that she was excited about her

making the soccer team?

What convinced the 'cool guys' to start attending the girls' soccer games?

If Sasha became rich, what would she buy?

ESSAY

What did Otto mean when he said that a player could 'see the field' while they are playing? Explain. Is Courtney one of these special players that can 'see the field'? Is Sasha?

Chapters 25-27

Why was goaltending in direct contrast to Sasha's 'natural instincts'?

Why was Otto impressed by the way in which Sasha tended the goal, even though a shot never came her way during practice? What did her style of goaltending teach the team?

By competing in a sport, Sasha found herself to be a changed person. How did playing soccer change her?

ESSAY

In Chapter 27, Sasha says that 'if you tell someone they are something good, they can be more of it.' Describe a time in your life when someone gave you a compliment that made you feel better about yourself, or a time when you gave someone else a compliment that made them feel better. What do compliments do for self-confidence? Is Sasha affected by Otto's compliments?

Chapters 28-30

What eventually happened to Shawna in Chapter 28 that enabled Sasha to become the starting goalkeeper?

Would you feel safe riding in a car with Clyde? Why or why not?

What does "Nagyon szepen Koszonom, Kosci" mean in Hungarian?

ESSAY

Name at least three of the people who came out to watch the big game against Franklin. Describe Sasha's relationship with each one of them. Who wasn't at the game? If you played in a big game, name three people in your life who would be there.

Chapters 31-33

What clue did Sasha notice in all those hours of shagging balls in practice that helped her make the save on Ashley Aiken's final kick?

What does Sasha mean when she says that 'people were gray?'

When Sasha stepped up to defend that final kick, she was overcoming her fears. Has there ever been a moment in your life when you overcame your fears? Explain.

ESSAY

Congratulations! You have completed another Scobre Press book! Sasha was afraid of everything when this book started. Eventually, she managed to overcome her fears. Has there ever been anything you were afraid of? How did you overcome your own fears? What did you learn from Sasha's journey?